TALON

DEVIL'S MURDER MC

USA TODAY BESTSELLING AUTHOR

NIKKI LANDIS

Cover by Pretty in Ink Creations

Model: Dylan Horsch

Image: FuriousFotog

Table of Contents

AUTHOR'S NOTE

Talon is the fourth book in the Devil's Murder MC.

It's filled with dark and gritty content, a supernatural twist, steamy scenes, violence, biker slang, torture, kidnapping, and forced proximity. Mature readers only. Heed the CWs and proceed with caution. Tough subjects occur in this book, please don't read if they will cause you discomfort.

I hope you enjoy Talon and Gail's story.

The series contains ongoing storylines and themes that may not be resolved in every book, but each couple will eventually receive their HEA.

COMMON TERMS

DMMC Devil's Murder Motorcycle Club. One-percenter outlaw MC with several chapters within the U.S. Founded in Henderson, NV 1981.

The Crow Shifter ability & shared soul of every Devil's Murder club member; a black feathered, predatory bird with enhanced traits.

Murder A group of crows, an omen of death.

Kraa An intense cry from a crow, fueled by strong emotion.

The Roost Bar & clubhouse owned by the Devil's Murder MC.

Bull's Saloon Second home to club members, bar owned by Lucky Lou.

Mobbing Individual crows assembling together to harass a rival or predator by cooperatively attacking it.

One-percenter Outlaw biker/club

Pres President of the club. His word is law.

Ol' lady A member's woman, protected wife status.

Cut Leather vest worn by club members, adorned with patches and club colors, sacred to members.

Church An official club meeting, led by president.

Chapel The location for church meetings in the clubhouse.

Prospect Probationary member sponsored by a ranking officer, banned from church until a full patch.

Full Patch A new member approved for membership.

Rook Former president, son of Jackdaw.

Crow Third generation club member, son of Rook, president.

Hog motorcycle

Cage vehicle

Muffler bunny Club girl, also called sweet butt, cut slut.

DDMC Dirty Death MC, rival motorcycle club.

TALON

PLAYLIST

Crows – Saliva

Echo – Trapt

Next Contestant – Nickelback

Something's Gonna Kill Me (Piano) – Corey Kent

Curiosity – Bryce Savage

Beggin' – Måneskin

Breathe – Kansh

Last Shot – Wesley Green

Devil You Know – Tim Montana

A Symptom Of Being Human – Shinedown

Dangerous Hands – Austin Giorgio

Already Over – Mike Shinoda

One Eyed Bastard – Green Day

Don't Let Me Down – HOSTAGE

Dynamite – Any Given Sin

You can find Nikki's Playlists on Spotify

TALON

⁚D E V I L'S M U R D E R M C⁚

Talon, Enforcer for the Devil's Murder MC, always puts the safety of the club and his brothers above everything else. He's used to establishing order and getting his knuckles bloody. His president, Crow, put him in charge of security along with the enforcement of club rules and regulations.

Talon never fails to get the job done. So, when Crow orders him to find and protect his sister, he doesn't hesitate. His tracker abilities and sharp instincts make him the perfect guy to get the job done. He never expects Abigail Holmes to be beautiful, sweet, and hunted by a ruthless enemy.

Now, Talon's protective, possessive nature has kicked in. No one is going to harm Gail. He's spent two months keeping her safe, watching from the shadows, and stalking the pretty brunette. But when her house is broken into and trashed, and he hears her scream, all bets are off.

He's done watching and waiting. Gail is his, and he doesn't care if Crow or anyone else tries to keep him from claiming the woman who's become his everything. His obsession may cost him his life or, worse, his position in the club. It's a risk he has to take. Talon's sole focus is keeping Gail safe, and he'll kill anyone who gets in his way.

Prologue

TALON

Two months earlier

THE SKY WAS FUCKING dark tonight. Black as sin. The moon hid behind gray clouds and stayed there as I sat on my Harley, staring at the address Eagle Eye texted me four hours ago. My ass hadn't moved since I arrived, planted on the seat of my bike while I waited for anyone to come home. Every window in the house across the street remained dark. Only two lights, one on the front porch and another above the carport illuminated the driveway and yard.

The quiet neighborhood seemed secure and low on crime. Crow's sister lived toward the end of her street on the left. This particular road had no outlet, so the traffic stayed minimal. It was easy for me to stake out the place since there was only one way in or out of the neighborhood.

My phone buzzed with an incoming text.

She home yet?

Nikki Landis

I shot back a quick, one-word reply. **No.**

Seven hours from my current location, my pres awaited information about his sister. The Roost, our clubhouse, resided in Henderson. He might as well have been next to me. I could feel his tension and worry, but the clear picture of him in my head, pacing inside his office, confirmed his feelings. He frowned, glancing at the crow that cawed outside his window. I chuckled when he lifted his hand, and his middle finger flipped me off. He knew I kept an eye on him.

Hell, I watched all my brothers. As Enforcer, that was my job. Protection. The safety of the club above everything else. I established order and got my knuckles bloody when force was needed. Lately, that was often. Crow put me in charge of security and the enforcement of club rules and regulations. I stood by his side and backed him up. Always.

But that wasn't why I could see him in his office.

We linked because of the crows—specifically, *my* crow.

Every member of the Devil's Murder MC connected with our crow. That bond varied for each member. My pres could control and lead the murder. They would form a mob for his bidding and attack on command. The V.P. Raven could call the crows to him whenever in need, a distress call that would rile them up and bring them ready for battle. His range stretched for miles. The Sergeant at Arms Hawk could take on the crow's form. If I had never seen his onyx wings, I probably would have doubted that he had the ability to transform partially. But he shifted into the crow on numerous occasions.

Me? I tapped into the crow's sight, and not just my own. I could communicate between them without words. Through the crows' eyes, I saw what *they* saw. I shared their feelings. Through them, I could briefly tap into the emotions of my brothers. A strange, empathic ability that combined with those visions and opened a channel between us. I couldn't read thoughts, but that didn't matter when I sensed the emotion behind them.

So, it wasn't hard to notice Crow's agitation and worry.

If I had any doubt, he didn't stay silent. Not that it was in his nature.

Crow texted every five fucking minutes.

What about now?

A sigh escaped as I grumbled under my breath. **Nothing yet.**

I tapped into my crow's sight and shook my head. My pres lit a smoke in his office and glared at the window. To fuck with him, I urged my crow to peck at the glass. Something left his hand and hit the pane, causing my crow to fly upward, landing on the roof as he squawked with irritation.

Laughing, I focused on the present, noticing the outdoor lights illuminating the yards and driveways on the street.

I stayed hidden in the shadows where I parked my bike, cracking my neck. Someone had to come home soon. It was late. The sun had set over an hour ago.

Headlights illuminated the darkened street as a vehicle approached, slowing before turning right and pulling onto the empty driveway across the street.

Here we go.

A pretty, ocean-blue Kia Seltos pulled to a stop as I waited for the driver to exit. The door opened, and I noticed long legs first. They went for fucking miles. *Goddamn.* I loved a tall woman. My greedy gaze devoured her, inch by inch, as she stood, bending over to reach inside and grab her purse. Tight denim clung to toned thighs and a thick ass. Fuckkkkk.

I hadn't even seen her face yet and knew I wanted, no *needed*, to be near this woman. I gripped the handlebars on my bike, leaning forward as my gaze raked over every inch of her body. She flipped her long brown hair over her shoulder, and I sucked in a breath, catching the slight jiggle of her ass as she shut the door with her hip.

I need closer.

Firing off a quick text to Crow, I let him know she arrived home.

His reply was so fast I knew he held his phone and watched the screen every minute until now.

Keep watch. Need her safe.

Got it, pres.

Until now, I had never focused on her name, but it left my lips in a whisper. "Abigail Holmes."

She entered her house, flipping on a light in the kitchen. I snuck to a window and peered inside, watching her drop her purse and keys on the countertop. It must have been a long day because she grabbed a glass and a bottle of red wine and poured, filling it before she took a long sip. Her head tilted back, and a soft sigh escaped.

Baby, I got all kinds of ways to help you relax.

She moved to the living room, kicking off her shoes and sinking onto the plush cream-colored couch that faced a flat-screen television. She never turned it on. The sexy goddess tucked in her feet as she relaxed against the seat. She drank the wine in less than fifteen minutes, setting the empty glass aside. Her eyes fluttered, and I couldn't help thinking she was far too vulnerable as they closed, and she sank further into the couch, asleep within a minute.

I didn't move from the shadows outside, creeping around her home, checking the perimeter, and switching vantage points for the next couple of hours. She never woke up.

When I heard her whimpering in her sleep, I rushed to the carport, testing the handle on her door. Unlocked. She fucking forgot to lock it. Didn't she know the danger she exposed herself to? Goddamn. I wanted to spank her luscious ass for this.

I let myself in, cautiously placing every step. To prevent anyone from sneaking up on her place without my knowledge, I called my crow. Outside, his soft caw confirmed he arrived with a few of his friends. I heard their soft chitters.

My gaze scanned the interior, noting the décor in shades of gray and white with rich, dark wood furniture.

4

She seemed to love plants and keeping everything clean. Spotless.

I couldn't resist moving closer, eager to see more of Abigail Holmes. Dropping to a crouch, I dared to move within touching distance.

Too fucking close, but I didn't care.

Light from the kitchen shined behind her, accentuating the golden hues in her silky brown hair. She frowned in her sleep, and a tiny crinkle appeared between her eyes before disappearing. I wished she would open them so I could see the shade. Would they be the same stormy gray as her brother?

I wasn't picky when it came to women. I loved their softness and curves, and I didn't care what color hair or eyes or what body type as long as they had an ass. I liked to feel a woman's thighs wrapped around me. But now, staring at the angelic face of Abigail Holmes, I became a fan of brunettes with long dark lashes, bubblegum pink lips, and pale, flawless skin.

My pulse picked up, and I grabbed my chest. How could she have such a hold over me before we ever spoke?

I wanted to know everything about this woman. Her passion for neatness. Why she loved plants. The reason she decided on a career as a pharmacy tech. Did she want to be a pharmacist? Her favorite food. Did she prefer tea or coffee? How did she take it?

Once I focused on her, I couldn't stop staring. In an instant, she became an obsession. I needed all the details. Her past. Her present. *Everyfuckingthing.*

Why was she kept apart from the club and her brother? Did Rook keep his distance, too? What kind of childhood did she have? Who raised her? Why didn't she know anything about the Devil's Murder MC?

What the fuck happened? Because Rook kept her hidden for a reason.

Caw...caw.

My head jerked upright, tearing my gaze from the beauty on the couch as I heard a branch snap outside. I moved toward the noise, staying low as I hugged the shadows and the perimeter walls. Crickets chirped outside, and I heard a cat hissing in the neighbor's yard. I caught movement outside on her lawn when I approached the nearest window.

Motherfucker!

Caw...caw.

The throaty rattle of my crow sounded distressed outside. He sensed my agitation but shared my concern.

No one should be outside Abigail's home this late at night.

I snuck outside, ordering half the crows to remain perched on her roof and ready to inform me if anyone else approached. The rest took to the sky, searching for any threat. A twig snapped to my right as I left the house, following the sound as footsteps proved someone trespassed. I rounded the corner, catching the silhouette of a man before he hopped her fence.

Shit!

The crows above me squawked with alarm as I raced across the lawn and climbed over the fence. I dropped to the ground and caught his hasty flight toward a black truck parked down the street. My boots pounded the pavement as I gave chase.

I didn't reach him before he threw open the door and started the engine, gunning it and almost running me over as he sped off. My body hit the ground as I rolled out of the way, diving toward the sidewalk to avoid being trampled. I searched the back of the truck and sighed when I didn't find a license plate. Of course not. That would be too fucking easy.

I pushed off the ground, tapping into my crow's vision as he followed the truck. He would keep going until the vehicle stopped. I didn't want to wait, so I ran back to Abigail's and slipped inside, annoyed that she still hadn't moved. She rested as if she knew I stood there, ready to guard her from any threat.

6

Her body shivered in her sleep, and I reached for the blanket folded over a nearby chair, gently sliding it over her as she snuggled into the cushions.

I felt this instant attraction combined with the knowledge that she needed protection, conjuring a fierce need to shelter Abigail from harm. Shit. If I had a type, it would be vulnerable women. But this time, it wasn't just about finding a stranger peeking through her windows or a boyfriend who couldn't control his fists. This woman was blood to my pres and family, which meant she was off limits. A biker princess with a whole club of outlaws to watch her back.

My head knew the right thing to do. *Keep my distance. Listen to my pres and follow orders.*

My heart? My cock? They both became consumed by her.

Fuck. I could feel that stalker mentality rising inside me—the need to keep every other male from what I wanted to claim as mine. I never even looked into her eyes or heard her voice, and I already knew I would kill for her. Fuck. I'd die for Abigail.

The crow felt the bond. He understood it. That feeling nudged me to wake and pull her into my embrace, swearing I would always be by her side.

Fucking strange.

Abigail mumbled in her sleep, and I missed the words, but restlessness, a hint of fear, and fatigue pushed through my mind. I froze. The breath in my lungs left as I exhaled, startled by the influx.

For the first time, I sensed emotion that didn't belong to me or my MC brothers. It originated from *her*.

How? No fucking clue.

But I felt what *she* felt, followed by a final wave of serenity and sweetness of spirit that could only belong to Abigail.

There was no possibility of keeping my distance after this. I was totally fucked.

Chapter 1

TALON

Present day

MY PHONE VIBRATED INSIDE my cut as I reached inside, tugging it free to glance at the screen.

Crow. *Again.*

Keep your distance. Don't want her spooked.

Yeah, I fucking knew. He didn't let me forget it.

On it, pres.

I was in a bad fucking mood. Abigail had gone on three dates this week, all with the same nerdy guy with thick glasses and a stare that always rested on her ass when she wasn't looking. The ass I wanted to fucking touch. The one I already considered *mine.* The timing sucked. Secrecy sucked.

I'd kept Crow informed and followed his instructions for eight goddamn weeks. I chased three masked men from her house on different occasions, but none of their vehicles had plates.

Not that it mattered since I sent the crows to follow. Always the same address. A pizza shop in downtown Carson City.

I scoped the place a few times while she went to work but couldn't get inside. The restaurant didn't seem to have the space for any hidden operation. Sending men to her house didn't make sense. Who the fuck wanted more information on her and why?

I sent a text to Eagle Eye. **Any news?**

Still digging.

The same fucking reply I got every time I asked. He'd run financials. The owner's info. Any known affiliations. It all came back squeaky clean. And that alone raised a red flag. No business was that legit. I knew Eagle Eye would keep working until something turned up; I just didn't have the fucking patience. I also didn't need to be blindsided by something that could get Abigail hurt.

Frowning, I almost growled as Abigail's date slipped his arm around her and led her to his car, opening the passenger door for her. She bent down to sit inside his Mustang, and he grinned like he knew he had an audience.

There go his eyes. Straight to her ass again. Fucker.

I couldn't help the churning in my gut and the worry that this could be related to the Dirty Death MC. Fucking Undertaker. Their pres caused a lot of fucking problems for our club that had nothing to do with our rivalry. He started the war with us and picked a goddamn fight when he could have left shit alone. But after he killed Rook, any hope of reaching a peaceful conclusion ended. Only his death would appease the club.

With a sigh, I scrubbed a hand down my face and over the scruff on my jaw, clenching my teeth when I saw the needle dick fucker driving Abigail to dinner.

If he touched her again, I would cut off any part of his body that dared to brush across her skin.

Mine, the crow reminded me. Yeah. I fucking heard it from him too.

The crow wanted to mate.

My pres warned me to leave his sister alone.

I followed the Mustang to a fucking Italian restaurant. One of those pricey ones with dark décor and romantic ambiance. He probably thought he would get lucky tonight. I'd set him straight.

I parked my bike and stalked the windows, finally stepping inside to snag a seat down the same aisle. Big menus sat on the table, and I held one up, blocking me from curious eyes. I waited until the guy got up to take a piss, and I followed him, entering behind him as he whipped out his dick at one of the stalls.

I couldn't help glancing at it. *Yep. Needle dick.*

He could never satisfy Abigail like I could.

When he zipped up, I rushed forward, slamming his body into the wall. He yelped as I pinned him in place, checking his pockets until I pulled out his wallet.

"What the fuck? Get off me!" He wasn't much of a threat, with his face smashed into the brown tile and his arms pinned behind him.

I scanned his license, memorizing the name and address before shoving it back to where I got it. "What do you want with Abigail Holmes?"

"What?"

I repeated the question, tightening my grip.

"I-I know her from work. I like her."

With a name like Harold Simpson, I figured he probably told the truth. He sounded like a pharmacist.

"You're gonna tell her you're not feeling well and end the date."

"Why would I do that?"

"Because I will fucking chop off your cock and shove it down your goddamn throat, needle dick. She's not yours to date, touch, or even fucking think about."

"Shit," he cursed. "I don't want trouble."

"This is your only chance to avoid it. Don't ask her out again."

"Fuck. Okay, man."

"I know where you live. Remember that."

I let him go as he stumbled from the stall, rushing toward the bathroom door. He didn't even look my way. I waited a couple of minutes before I followed, exiting the restaurant in time to catch the Mustang as it left the lot with Abigail inside. I sent the crows ahead of me as I fired up my bike, following them at a safe distance. I bet he watched that rearview mirror the entire way to Abigail's house.

A smirk twitched my lips. *Don't touch what's mine, asshole.*

Harold didn't waste time dropping her off. The fucker didn't even make sure she got inside the house before he backed down the driveway and pressed on the gas, skidding in his haste. Abigail shook her head as she entered her home, and I parked my bike in the usual spot, cutting the engine.

Harold Simpson didn't get it. A woman like her was worth fighting over. She was perfect in every way. I noticed the organized way she arranged her clothes in her closet and cleaned the house every weekend. How she never forgot to water her plants. I trailed behind her when she went shopping, always at the same grocery store every Saturday.

She put effort into her appearance even when she only planned to buy groceries. Hair and makeup done in case one of her friends invited her to something last minute. Hell, maybe she wanted more dates. I wouldn't let it happen, but I could understand loneliness.

And that was the emotion I felt from her more than any other.

That familiar ache in the chest. A yearning for something more. We both shared it.

Later that night, with the crows watching from her roof, I slid under her bed. From here, I could feel the rise and fall of her chest like it sank into mine and slightly hovered above it. As if we shared every inhalation and exhalation, breathing in tandem. I wanted to slide out and pull back her sheets, letting her body heat and mine collide.

My eyes closed as my hands lowered, silently unbuckling my belt and popping the button on my jeans. I unzipped with such careful restraint that I nearly groaned when my cock finally sprang free. I suppressed a guttural cry of pleasure when my fist wrapped around my cock, slowly stroking the length as I imagined sliding into Abigail's pussy and that first delicious plunge inside her wet heat.

"Mmmm," she breathed above me as I heard the mattress creak.

I froze. Did she hear me?

A moan followed, and I shivered as I realized she was doing the same thing above me as I did right now. Touching herself. Getting off. Growing excited.

She needed release. Fuckkkk.

I imagined her legs falling open and her thighs parting wide. How her legs would tremble as her fingers dipped inside her tight cunt. The sticky, slick sweetness of her arousal. Was she bare? Did she leave a strip on her mound?

I needed to know. How could I have the right daydreams if I never saw her pretty pussy? Every woman in my past vanished from my head. I didn't want to imagine a single fucking thing about Abigail. I had to learn it. Memorize it. Use my teeth, lips, and tongue to map out her entire body and every inch of her skin, all the dips and valleys, every curve, the musk that settled between her legs, and the taste of her climax.

I heard a slight vibration and buzzing sound and knew what she powered on.

Naughty girl.

She might get off that way tonight, but I wouldn't let her come without me for long. The creaking of the mattress increased. Her breathy moans grew louder. I could swear her heels dug into the bed.

Fuck. I wanted her.

She fucking turned me on. Lust fogged my brain.

I kept stroking, tugging harder and faster, moving my hips only enough to cause friction. The denial collided with the need pulsing in my veins.

I knew when she came. Her soft cry echoed in the room. Not to be left behind, I followed, pumping into my fist and unable to control where I spurted as ropes of my cum landed on my stomach and shot onto the underside of her mattress. Like the sick fuck that I was, I felt satisfaction that I marked her bed with a part of me.

My body trembled with the force of that orgasm, and I knew it would be a hundred times better when I came inside her pussy. This would have to do for now.

I smeared the sticky fluid across the underside of the bed and let it dry, enjoying the thought I had claimed her in some small way. I used the bottom of my shirt to wipe myself clean and pushed my semi-hard cock back inside my pants. I needed to avoid touching myself for a bit to build up the anticipation.

Abigail's deep, even breaths soon followed. She fell asleep.

I slowly finished snapping my jeans closed and buckling my belt. I slid from under her bed, standing over her as I noted the serene expression on her face. I longed to see her sated like this after I fucked her for most of the night.

She rolled onto her side and faced me as her lips parted. I knelt at the side of her bed, toying with the idea of rubbing my thumb over the surface.

The sudden urge to lean closer and brush my lips over hers consumed me.

I nearly took what I wanted but shook my head and pulled back.

I didn't want a single thing she didn't give me freely.

Forcing myself to walk out her door, I left to roam the perimeter of the house, hoping the night air would cool the heat on my skin. But it didn't stop my thoughts from focusing on the sexy woman inside. How would she taste on my tongue and feel beneath my fingertips?

The next morning, I followed her to work. I told myself I needed that energy drink and wouldn't walk by the pharmacy—a lie. I hung around in an empty aisle, watching as she cashed out customers. She always wore a smile.

Abigail never got impatient or tried to rush anyone. This woman was so fucking sweet I wondered if she should be brought into the life of a crow. Being a biker ol' lady was tough. Some women weren't cut out for it. Crow knew that firsthand. His mom split when shit got hard with the club.

But Abigail had Holmes blood. She was born into it whether Rook kept her hidden or not. And just because Crow's mother couldn't hack it, it didn't mean the same for Abigail. It sure got me curious about what kind of life she had before now. How was it possible she never learned about her brother or the motorcycle club that meant everything to her father?

I checked out at the front of the store and headed to my bike, chugging the energy drink before I rode out of the lot. My head was a fuckin' mess, and I went for a ride to clear it, arriving an hour before her shift was scheduled to end.

That night, I stayed outside and didn't enter the house. I had to get this possessive urge to claim her out of my system. Crow would fucking kill me if he knew how far I had gone already, testing the limits and pushing boundaries.

I had it under control. . .until ten days later when everything went to shit.

Chapter 2

TALON

Aɴᴏᴛʜᴇʀ ᴄᴏᴄᴋsᴜᴄᴋᴇʀ sʜᴏᴡᴇᴅ ᴜᴘ to take Abigail on a date.

Unfuckingbelievable.

Where did these guys come from? Did she have an account on every dating app in town? I didn't get it. After I got rid of Harold, three more showed up to take his place.

The first guy took off when he saw me stalking his way in my leather cut. He never made it to her door. I thought for sure Abigail saw me, but she didn't.

The second fucker managed to take her to a movie. I met him outside the theater when he went for more popcorn and escorted his ass outside. He didn't bother coming back. I followed her home after she called an Uber and hoped that was the end of it.

Nope.

Asshole number three now had her in his truck and parked next to an adult arcade. I had to admit it was a creative way to get to know someone. Everyone loved playing games.

I had a few of my own that I played with deadly accuracy.

She called the third guy Nick. I thought he treated her the best until I saw him admiring her tits as she rolled balls underhanded at the targets while playing Skee-Ball. That pissed me off.

As soon as I could get to him, I closed in, pushing him around the corner and out of view. Agitated, I shoved him against the wall next to the bathroom, nearly cutting off his airway with the fake leather jacket he wore. My lips curled into a snarl. "You're gonna leave. Now."

He glared at me. "Fuck you."

"You sure you want to say that to me? Look at my cut."

He frowned before his gaze swept over me, landing on my patch. "Shit."

"You ever heard of the Devil's Murder MC?"

He swallowed. "Yeah."

"Abigail Holmes is under our protection. You don't talk to her. You don't date her. And you sure as fuck don't touch what's mine."

"Fuck, man." He cleared his throat. "Yeah. Got it."

I didn't care for his attitude. "Get lost."

He stomped away after I released him, shaking his head and muttering about bikers. Like, I gave a fuck about his opinion.

I considered this a win until I walked outside, dropped onto the seat of my Harley, and noticed Abigail's devastated expression. She couldn't see me, but she did catch Nick leaving her stranded at the Arcade.

Shit.

She sat at a table for thirty minutes. Alone.

She didn't go home either. I saw her call someone, swiping at her face and the tears that fell. My hand clutched at my chest. I felt the pain. The fucking heartache.

What right did I have to keep her from being happy?

Caw...caw.

The crows landed on the roof and hopped around, croaking as they felt the tension rolling off my shoulders. One of the bolder ones belted a throaty kraa.

I sighed as I watched Abigail, wondering if I should back off when a car pulled up, staying hidden in the shadows. Unmarked. No plate. Black with tinted windows so dark I couldn't see inside. A window rolled down, and I spotted the cigarette tossed outside, landing on the asphalt with a spray of cinders.

The brief flash of light illuminated the face I had just met. Nick. Her fucking *date*.

Why the fuck was he watching her right now? Unease coiled in my gut. Something wasn't right.

He sped off as Abigail stood and walked toward the entrance. A car pulled up and parked, honking the horn as she exited. The driver waved. A blonde who worked with Abigail. A friend I saw her visit on multiple occasions outside of work.

Relieved, I hung back and waited for the car to leave. I followed them for a few miles until they stopped at a diner. Once they were seated, I dialed Eagle Eye's number.

"What you need, Talon?"

"I've got a tail on Abigail. First name Nick. No last name. He took her on a date, and I sent him packin'."

Eagle Eye snorted. "You want to know who he is?"

"Yeah. After he left the arcade on Main and 5th, he showed up in a different vehicle than he left in. Think you can use cameras from the area and do some facial rec?"

"I'm almost insulted, Talon."

"Don't fuck with me, brother. Something about the guy set off my crow."

"Shit. I'll get right on it."

"Thanks."

I ended the call and lit a smoke, keeping myself hidden from the women. Not that it mattered. It was too bright inside the diner and too fucking dark out here.

Still, I didn't want to be spotted.

The women stayed for two hours. I stood and stretched, giving my tired, aching muscles a brief workout in the cool air. Fatigue pressed in, and I ignored the urge to shut my eyes for a few minutes. I wouldn't risk leaving Abigail vulnerable or unprotected.

My phone vibrated with an incoming call, and I swiped across when I saw Eagle Eye's name. "That didn't take long."

"Because Nick Grime doesn't hide who he is or what he does for a living."

"And that is?" I asked, growing impatient.

"Hired thug. Got pinched twice last year for assault. He likes to rough people up for money. He works his business from that fucking pizza place you told me about. He's good at hiding his shit, but not better than me."

"Fuck. What does he want with Crow's sister?"

"That's for you to sort, brother."

"Anything else I need to know?"

"Yeah. Watch your back. Nick has been spotted with Dirty Death MC members."

Son of a bitch! "I'll watch mine *and* Abigail's."

"Good." He cleared his throat. "Listen. Nick's got a cousin who works for the sheriff's department. He's an inside guy. Name is Luke Grime. Apart they're trouble. Together they're fucking deadly."

"They won't get the jump on me."

He chuckled. "Never doubted that."

"Keep digging, Eagle Eye. We need to find out as much about these Grime fuckers as we can. There's a reason Nick tried to get close to Crow's sister."

"Already on it. Gonna give this info to Crow."

"Understood."

"I'll be in touch." He hung up.

Crow texted me thirty minutes later after Abigail arrived back home. **She safe?**

I didn't bother replying with a text and called him instead.

The line didn't finish the first ring before he answered. "Talon."

"She's safe."

A sigh followed. "Heard about Nick and Luke Grime. You see either of them since the arcade?"

"No. I hope it stays that way."

"You get her out of there if shit goes down."

"I hear you, pres."

"If you think she's in danger, leave Carson City, even if she tries to fight you on it."

"I will," I promised.

The line went quiet before I heard Crow clear his throat. "She seem happy?"

"For the most part, yeah."

"Good."

I almost asked him what else was on his mind but decided against it. He still had to work through all the mental shit from his father's murder and the shock of learning he had a sister.

21

Add in Undertaker and the need for vengeance, and I could understand all the emotions clogging his mind. I fucking felt that shit, even through the phone.

"If anything happens, I'm the first to know. Not Eagle Eye. Not Raven. Me. You got that, Talon?"

"Yeah, pres, I do."

"She's all the blood I got left. You feel me?"

I did. "She's family, Crow. My life for hers." I meant it.

An outsider might not understand the oath I just made or its significance, but Crow did. "I won't forget this."

I made that promise as his brother, his friend, and a member of his family. The Devil's Murder was more than a motorcycle club. The bond we shared was unbreakable, as deep and infinite as the one we shared with the crows.

"Gotta run. I'll be in contact, pres."

"Stay sharp," he growled, ending the call.

I pocketed my phone, focusing on my only duty: protecting Abigail. Dawn began to creep over the horizon, and I knew I would have to leave the yard before anyone saw me. I didn't need nosy neighbors cocking this up. Or worse, someone calling the goddamn sheriff's office.

Before I left, I checked on Abigail. She slept peacefully, a small smile tugging on her lips. I wanted to know what she dreamed about, what secret fluttered in her heart, and why she suddenly seemed to relax as soon as I approached, like she could sense I was there.

The connection between us was real. I didn't imagine it.

The crow knew. I knew. And soon. . . Abigail would know, too.

"FUCK," I CURSED, BOUNCING my leg as I waited for Crow's sister to exit the pharmacy where she worked. Her shift should have ended about ten minutes ago, and she usually left right on the dot. I never saw her stay late. It wasn't needed. The pharmacy was fully staffed.

My thoughts centered on the last two months and all that happened since Crow learned about Abigail. The late nights. All her dates. Those asshole Grime cousins. None of that mattered when I stared into the stormy gray eyes that matched her brother's. She had become my entire focus.

For the last few days, I stayed vigilant, watching over her as my pres asked. He texted that he didn't want me to interfere in Abigail's life. His pops had kept her a secret, and none of us knew why. Rook, our dead former pres, should have told his son if no one else, but he didn't.

He died with that knowledge.

But then an envelope arrived with Rook's handwriting, addressed to Crow, and documents enclosed with Crow's sister's name on them, and Crow had to know if she was alive. I couldn't deny my new pres. Anything he wanted, hell, anything the fucking Holmes family needed, I wouldn't hesitate to provide. I owed them that fucking much. And it wasn't just Rook and Crow.

Patching into the Devil's Murder saved my life.

So, I didn't hesitate to ride to the address Eagle Eye provided and find Abigail Holmes. It turned out she was thriving, fucking *beautiful*, and living in Carson City. From what I could see, she had a good life here. She seemed happy.

Well, other than the night I ran off Nick.

I hadn't left Carson City since Crow sent me here, and I couldn't lie to myself that the gig wasn't a good one. I got to spend my time stalking a sexy brunette, and I didn't have to do shit but ensure she got to where she was going each day safely.

I stood outside for half an hour, agitated as fuck, until Abigail appeared. Her expression explained it. She'd had a rough day, and it showed. My chest constricted as I watched her sag against the driver's side door of her ocean-blue Kia Seltos, heaving a sigh and brushing a tear from her cheek.

Someone made her cry. Fuck.

My hands clenched. My heart pounded. Rage simmered under my skin. They. Would. Pay. As soon as I found out what happened, I'd find the motherfucker who dared to upset her.

I tailed the SUV to her house, parking down the street like I did every night. Jogging to her place, I crept among the shadows, watching her park underneath the carport.

I should have noticed something was off.

The crows landed on her roof, cawing like mad.

When I heard her scream, all bets were off. I didn't care about my orders. I didn't give a fuck who I pissed off. If someone were hurting that sweet girl, I would enjoy ripping them apart and the crows feasting on their organs.

Rushing inside the door underneath the carport, I entered the house. My gaze bounced all over, finding the mess someone left behind. All the tipped-over furniture and shit spilled everywhere. Broken pots that held her plants. Slashes through her couch. Glass from shattered light fixtures.

She crouched and hid, trembling as she turned on me with wide, frightened eyes. I could swear she assessed me with open curiosity. . .and appreciation.

But when she saw the gun in my hand, she gasped.

Well, fuck. I just screwed this up.

Chapter 3

GAIL

SOMEONE BROKE INTO MY house.

And that wasn't the worst. No, they *destroyed* my stuff. My plants and their expensive pots. My designer couch. The new light fixtures I replaced four months ago and saved for half a year to purchase. Who the hell would do that? Why?

I didn't have a lot of money. I barely scraped by and paid the bills on time. There wasn't some huge savings account I hid or wealthy family members to demand a ransom from. This didn't make any sense.

My back door slammed shut, and I realized I stood in my living room, in the open, without a way to protect myself. I took two steps toward my bedroom and my purse when I heard the door open again and slam shut a second time. I couldn't control my reaction.

I screamed. Not some sissy scream, either. This was scream-queen-worthy and left my throat hoarse when I finished.

Oh, God.

Was someone inside my house?

I could swear the walls rumbled as my carport door swung open and crashed against the wall. Frightened, confused, and exhausted from the mentally draining day, I crouched behind the couch. *Stupid.* That wouldn't stop the intruder from locating me.

The scent alerted me I wasn't alone first. A raw mixture of leather, motor oil, and mint hard candy. My eyes closed as I breathed the aroma in, nearly screaming again when I heard the floorboards creak. My eyes snapped open as I spotted the man who stood several feet away from me.

The stranger towered over my position as he glanced in my direction, scanned my body, and shifted his focus. His gaze tore away from me, darting around the room as if he expected some knife-wielding sicko to jump at him from the shadows.

I never had a chance to turn on all my lights yet. The hazy glow from my kitchen draped his body and provided the perfect backdrop. He was sin personified and built like a brick wall and indestructible. Tall, broad, with Nevada sun-kissed skin covered in dark ink, he swung his head in my direction.

A black t-shirt molded to his skin stretched over his biceps and pressed against the taught muscles of his abdomen. The kind of physique that wasn't big enough for bodybuilder status but definitely sculpted in all the right ways. His jeans struggled to contain his powerful thighs as I realized too late that my eyes followed down his body, taking in every inch of virile man. It took only a second for me to see that the bulge between his legs hung thick and low, slightly to the right. . .oh God.

I pulled my gaze from the sight as I felt a blush rising in my cheeks, flushing with mortification. It didn't stop me from lifting higher, taking in that expansive chest, and finally climbing to his face.

His short, auburn beard clung to his strong jaw. I couldn't believe how undeniably sexy he was, especially when I noticed his full lips that twitched with amusement.

But his eyes were what did me in, fluttering my heart when mine made contact. I instantly got lost in the piercing, crystal blue color that reminded me of the sea under a calm, cloudless sky. So pretty and yet still masculine. I barely took in his short, reddish-blond hair cut in that messy style that I usually found unattractive, but on him, it was *perfect*. He cleared his throat.

Neither of us said a word.

He stared at me in response, looking me over in a way that had me thinking about every impure sexual fantasy I'd ever conjured late at night in my bed. *Yum*.

What the hell was the matter with me?

I shouldn't be checking out a man who entered my home uninvited and probably wanted to kill me. Metal gleamed from a hard object in his hand as the light glinted off the surface.

Oh my God, he had a gun.

A noise like a mewl left my throat as I scrambled away, falling on my ass as I backed into the wall, terrified he was one of those home invasion types that didn't leave any witnesses behind.

His brows furrowed. "Fuck," he growled, his voice deep and raspy, as hard and dark as his thunderous expression. "Is anyone inside?"

"I-I don't know," I replied honestly, terrified that he wasn't the only intruder.

"I won't hurt you. I'm here to keep you safe."

My jaw popped open in shock as he moved with lethal grace, cutting off my chance to reply as he crept through every room in my house, pausing to check outside in both my backyard and the carport.

Only when he turned up back in my living room, alone, did I begin to think maybe he wasn't connected to whoever broke in.

"I shut the back door. It was swinging in the wind. I swear, I'm only here to protect you."

"You-you have a gun," I stuttered.

"Yeah, baby. I do. And I'll use it on any motherfucker stupid enough to try to hurt you."

I blinked, staring at the man in confusion. "Who are you?"

"That's a long answer with a lot of explanation. I'll tell you, but not right now. We have to leave."

I stood on shaky limbs, my hands slapping the wall as I steadied myself. "I can't leave my house with a stranger."

Even a handsome one.

"Is it the gun?" he asked with a growl.

Outside, I heard birds. Tons of them. They sounded like crows.

"Maybe," I replied, moving a few steps away as he took one in my direction.

"My name is Talon. I'm an enforcer for the Devil's Murder MC. Ever heard of my club?"

A biker club. I shook my head.

He cursed. "Okay. This is more complicated than I anticipated." He placed the gun behind his back, tucking it into his waistband. His hands lifted as if that alleviated all my anxiety and fear. "Babe. I need you to listen. You aren't safe."

No shit. I figured that out by myself.

"I know," I answered. Did he think I was stupid?

"Fuck." His gaze roamed my face. "Abigail Holmes."

My first and last name rolled off his tongue like he had said it a hundred times before.

"You're under the protection of my club. I was sent here to keep you safe. I've been watching over you for two months now. That's way more information than we have time for right now."

Two months?

Wait. He knew my name.

My fingers trembled as I pushed my hair out of my eyes. "I-I don't know," I faltered. My knees gave out, and I slid down the wall as Talon rushed to my side.

"Fuck. You're in shock."

"Don't hurt me," I whimpered as he crouched in front of me, lifting his hand to brush his knuckles across my cheek. That touch, so light and controlled, couldn't belong to someone who intended to kill me. Right?

"I already told you, beautiful. I'm here to protect you. Nothing more."

He called me beautiful. I stared into his eyes, searching for the truth. He held my gaze.

"You need to trust me. Your life depends on it."

"I'm terrified," I admitted.

"I know, and I'm gonna do everything I can to help you. I swear to fuck I'll answer all your questions, but we need to leave. You can't stay here."

"Where are you taking me?"

"To a safe house. No one can find you there."

"A safe house?" I asked, frowning as his words sank in. *No one can find you.*

Fuck. That.

I did the only thing I could think of, self-preservation kicking in as I slowly lifted my hands, placing them against his chest. Our eyes remained locked as my palm rested over his heart, startled by how hard it thumped beneath my hand.

Before he could guess what I intended, I shoved as hard as I could, knocking him backward. He fell on his ass, surprised I managed to unseat him. A growl rumbled his chest as I scrambled to my feet, running toward my room. I reached it before he did, slamming the door shut and turning the lock before racing for my purse.

I never considered the fact that we weren't alone. I figured whoever broke into my house would have left already. That proved a mistake.

A gun cocked as I froze, staring into dark eyes and down the barrel of a weapon that would obliterate me before I had a chance to blink.

The man wore a dark ski mask and dressed all in black.

Oh. Shit.

I should have trusted the biker and stayed with him. Wait. Didn't he just check to be sure we were alone? How did this intruder get inside without either of us noticing? Were we that caught up in one another?

How strange.

Talon banged on the door, and I jolted. "I know you're scared, Abigail. Fuck. Open up."

"I think we'll let him join our game. Open the door," the masked man ordered with a voice so familiar I could swear this wasn't a stranger.

I slowly turned and walked to the door, flipping the lock and opening it as Talon stood there, his body poised for action. "Help," I whispered.

He already palmed his gun, aiming at the masked man behind me. "I've got you," he promised.

After this, I believed Talon told the truth.

Caw. . .caw.

A crow pecked at the panes of glass at my window.

Another joined him, and another, until so many black wings flapped that I lost count. Why were they gathering like that? They would break my window!

The masked guy was startled and shifted his gaze. In that single heartbeat, Talon reacted with a calm, swiftness that I didn't know was possible. He fired, hitting the intruder in the chest. Twice. I watched the bullets strike his body and throw him backward with force. Blood began pumping from the wounds as he coughed and sputtered. Crimson fluid dripped from the corner of his mouth.

So much blood.

I covered my ears and screamed, making myself tiny as I lowered to the floor. This couldn't be real. Was I having a nightmare?

Panicked and frightened, I tried to reach my bed and my purse, scrambling toward it on my hands and knees. I had to leave! I needed to run!

Arms slid around my waist from behind and tugged as my back met a hard, muscled chest. "Shhh," Talon soothed. "You're okay. You're safe."

I sagged against him as my fingers gripped his arm. "Talon," I whimpered. "He's dead."

"I know, beautiful. I'm gonna make this better. Promise." His head turned, and his lips brushed my temple. "Will you trust me?"

I didn't have much of a choice. My home had been invaded. My belongings were trashed. I didn't know who hunted me or why. For a few seconds, I debated calling the police but decided against it.

What could they do? How long would it take for help to arrive?

I would just end up with a police officer for protection, and I knew that wasn't as reliable as the man who held me. A biker outlaw stood a better chance against the hitmen sent from an unknown enemy.

"I can try."

"That's good enough for now," he conceded, helping me to my feet. Two of his fingers grasped my chin. "I want you to keep your eyes on me or the door. That's it. Don't look down. Okay?"

I nodded, shaking as adrenaline coursed through me. "My purse."

"I've got it. You need anything else?"

"My thyroid pills and phone charger."

He reached for my hand and pulled me against his side, slipping my purse over my shoulder and across my body. He dumped my charger, medication, and phone inside my handbag, then walked into the bathroom, dumping makeup, deodorant, and other essential items into the travel bag he found under the sink after he completed a quick search.

He paused to pick up my keys and shut off the lights on the way out. Talon locked the door after leading me outdoors and dropped them into my purse.

"There's one more thing you need to know before we ride off."

"I don't think I can take much more," I admitted, swaying on my feet.

He held me steady. "I know, baby, but this is important. The reason my club is looking out for you is because you have a brother—"

I gasped.

"—and he's the president."

Chapter 4

TALON

I DIDN'T ASK IF she'd ever ridden on a motorcycle before. It wasn't hard to figure out. She stared at my Harley like she thought it would roar to life and run her over with a mind of its own.

"Abigail—"

"Gail," she corrected.

"Gail, baby, we've got to go." I placed her travel bag inside my saddlebags and closed them. "Just hop on behind me and hold on tight. Don't let go for any reason. Alright?"

She stared at me, lost in her head. I could see the fog in her eyes and the way she swayed. She wouldn't last long. I had to reach one of the motels the club used or risk exposure, and that wasn't an option.

"I have a brother. A biker president."

"Yeah," I softly replied. "You do. Come on, Gail."

I threw a leg over the seat and fired up my bike, reaching out my hand.

She blinked. "Am I going to meet him?"

"When it's safe, yes."

"Talon?"

"Yeah, beautiful?"

"I think I'm going to pass out."

Fuck!

I climbed off the bike in a rush and caught her right before her head hit the ground. My body wrapped around hers, instantly seeking to comfort her, when I realized the shock had become too much. I should have waited to tell her about Crow.

It felt like an eternity had passed before she woke.

Gail moaned. Her lips parted as she whispered my name. "Talon."

"I'm here, baby."

Her eyes remained closed. "I'm dizzy."

"We can wait until you're ready," I promised, sending a message to my crow. I heard the caws that followed as they took to the sky, wings flapping hard to ensure no one else surprised us at Abigail's house.

If I weren't so caught up in her, I would have realized Nick snuck inside. Yeah, I figured out who it was as soon as he spoke. The fucker came back to hurt Gail, and I wasn't sorry I popped him twice for the effort. Too bad I didn't have a chance to let the crows in. That would have been enjoyable to watch.

For the second time today, I gave into the impulse and touched her face, lightly stroking her soft cheek with my finger. "So beautiful," I murmured, momentarily forgetting how that would sound to her.

She blinked. Gray eyes focused on my face. Framed by thick dark lashes, they stared into my soul.

"Why are you looking at me like that?"

Shit. "Like what?"

"Like you *know* me. Like we've spoken a thousand times, and you're invested in helping me." She frowned. "You really did watch over me for two months, didn't you?"

With a nod, I confirmed it.

"But this is more."

I didn't say shit to that. "Are you still dizzy?"

She sighed. "No."

"Then we need to head out." I helped her up, placing my hands on her hips as I led her to my bike, refusing to release her until her sexy ass planted on my seat. Not wasting time, I slipped my helmet over her head, buckling the strap beneath her chin. I'd ride without one to ensure she was protected. I pulled my leather jacket out of the saddlebags and helped her into it, zipping it up to her chin.

Her bare legs were too exposed, but that would have to wait. At least she had a pair of Nike's on.

"Will my brother meet us somewhere?"

Once I took my place in front of her, I looked over my shoulder. "Not sure yet. Slide your arms around my waist and hold on. It's gonna be a long ride."

"Okay."

"If you feel too tired to hold on, you tap my thigh. If you need *anything*, tap my thigh. It'll get my attention fast."

"I can do that."

We left Carson City and rode toward Tonopah. I could stop at The Crossroads if I sensed we were being followed, so I didn't worry about the ride. The Tonopah Royal Bastards always had a place for a member of the Devil's Murder MC and vice versa.

Tonopah was the halfway point to Henderson. A good place to lay low if we could get there without Luke Grime or any of the Dirty Death following us. At some point, Crow would want to meet his sister, and it seemed a good idea to have that exchange take place before she got overwhelmed by the entire club.

After about an hour, Gail's hands kept slipping. She rested against my back as the wind whipped around us, and I knew it was more than the cold air causing her fatigue. She'd never make it to Tonopah. Not tonight.

I figured the safe house in Hawthorne would work better than Tonopah if we could reach it but that didn't happen either. I wasn't willing to risk her falling off my bike.

We rolled up to a motel outside Lux. I had stayed here a few times on runs for the club, so I knew the owner. I parked my bike and brought Gail with me to secure a room, then rode around the back where no one could see my Harley from Hwy 95.

We entered after I swiped the key, bringing all our belongings from my saddlebags, which wasn't much. I kept a travel bag like she had and an extra change of clothes. Nothing else.

"Why don't you take a shower?" I suggested after dropping my bags on the only table in the room. "It'll help after the long ride."

She nodded with a weary smile. "Okay."

"I've got an extra t-shirt you can change into if you want." I reached inside my bag and tugged it free, walking to her as I passed the shirt into her hand. "You need anything else?"

Her teeth nibbled on her bottom lip. "I need to eat something. All I've had today is a granola bar and yogurt for breakfast."

Damn. That was nothing. "How about I order food while you shower? What's your favorite?"

"In-N-Out Burger."

I slapped a hand over my heart. "I'm in love."

She giggled, then frowned. "I need protein. A chicken sandwich and iced tea. No sugar. Onion rings but no onions on anything."

That wasn't hard to remember. "You got it, beautiful."

Gail shut the door after she entered the bathroom, and I heard the lock click into place. It didn't offend me. She didn't know who the fuck I was, and she was scared. A lot happened today for her to absorb and come to terms with. We'd have to talk over dinner.

I found a place that delivered lunch items any time of the day or night, and I placed an order first, then dialed Crow's number.

"Talon." He sounded anxious.

"Nick Grime broke into Gail's place and trashed it. I'm not sure if he worked alone."

"Fuck!"

"She's okay. I've got her, pres."

"Goddammit. Is she alright?"

"Physically, yeah, but she's confused and scared. I had to tell her who I was and why I was there before she would let me help her."

Crow grunted. "Yeah. That makes sense."

"I told her she had a brother, and he's the club president. That's why I was sent to protect her. She's gonna have questions."

"Sure, she is," he agreed. "She isn't dumb. Abigail is a Holmes. That blood runs in her veins. She's probably gonna get pissed when the shock wears off."

"Yeah, pres, and that's not all. I had to take out Nick. He aimed his gun at her, and I fired before he had a chance. She's shaken up."

Crow cursed, and I held the phone away from my ear until he calmed down.

"Fucking motherfuckers. I'm sending a cleanup crew."

"He fucked up her furniture and plants. I think she's upset. I didn't see Luke. He's in the wind, but I don't know how long. I don't think we've got a tail, but I'll keep watch. Anything looks suspicious, and I'm going dark."

"After you check in with me," he ordered.

"Of course, pres."

"You remember the safe house locations?"

"Yep."

"Where are you now?"

"That motel outside Lux. We'll lay low and rest until dark, then head toward Tonopah."

"I'll give Grim a call and let him know we might need his help."

"Good call." I paused. "She looks like you," I added, giving him that detail even though he didn't ask. "Same gray eyes and dark hair. She's a Holmes."

Crow cleared his throat. I sensed his struggle and the emotion entangled with it. "Check in with me before you head out."

"Will do, pres."

"One more thing."

"Yeah?"

"Keep your cock in your fucking pants. Touch my sister, and I'll rip off your fucking dick," Crow threatened.

Damn. "I hear you, pres."

We ended the call a few seconds before someone knocked on our door. I moved the curtains aside, peeking out as I palmed my gun. The delivery guy shuffled his feet, holding onto our bags of food and drinks. To be safe, I shrugged out of my cut and draped it over one of the chairs.

I tucked my gun behind my back and opened the door, taking the order and giving him a chin lift. "Thanks."

The guy spun on his heel and left, climbing into an old truck before he pulled away from the curb. I scanned the lot and nearby rooms. Nothing felt off.

I ordered my crow to watch my bike and the room and knew he would sound the alarm if anyone approached.

Crow's words echoed in my head. *Touch my sister, and I'll rip off your fucking dick.*

He didn't know what she meant to me. I didn't want to explain that shit over the phone. Gail wasn't some quick fuck. I didn't want to use her just to get my dick wet, even if my thoughts were consumed with lust and desire for this woman.

I knew, I fucking *knew* she was mine.

That was a huge problem because crows. . .mated for *life.*

The bathroom door opened as I set the food on the bed. I turned and locked the door before my gaze swung in her direction.

Fuck. Me.

Gail wore my t-shirt. . . and that was *all* she fucking wore. I knew because she draped her underwear and bra over the sink to dry. Her shorts and shirt were folded to the side.

Don't think about her pussy. Her soft, exposed, naked pussy.

Instant. Hard-on.

I struggled to breathe as my hand indicated the food had arrived. "Hungry?" The word came out strangled, but she didn't react.

Gail nodded, walked to the bed, and sat on the mattress. Her long legs lifted, exposing her upper thighs. Goddamn. She had the longest, sexiest legs.

I didn't dare glance toward the mirror because if I did and saw her ass, I'd be done for. I'd have to touch her, and that wouldn't end well.

Fuck. I swallowed the saliva in my mouth before I fucking drooled.

"What did you get?"

I joined her on the bed, opened the two bags, and lifted everything out. She'd get the first pick. I'd eat whatever she didn't.

"I ordered a couple of different chicken sandwiches since I wasn't sure if you wanted a deluxe or not. Every sauce on the menu for dipping. Onion rings and fries. A loaded double burger. Two fish sandwiches. And a couple of hot apple pies."

She blinked. "That's a lot of food."

I watched as she poked a straw in her tea and took a sip.

"I eat a lot."

"I can see that. This tea is perfect."

Without sugar? Disgusting. I didn't give her my opinion, though.

"Dig in." I reached for a fish sandwich and unwrapped it, taking a bite and chewing as I watched her check both chicken sandwiches, picking the one with the lettuce, tomato, pickle, and mayo.

"I'll take this one." She opened a ketchup and dunked an onion ring, avoiding the spicy sauce that came with them.

I cataloged all her choices in my mind so I would know what she wanted next time without having to ask.

"Tell me about your thyroid." Yeah, it was blunt, but I wanted to know how it affected her and why she needed medication for it.

"It's underactive. Hypothyroid, to be exact. I'm fine as long as I take my medication every day."

"And if you don't?"

"I get tired, like *really* tired, and it messes with my sleep. Sometimes it affects my heartrate too."

"Fuck, Gail." She wouldn't be missing any medication. Not on my watch.

"It sounds worse than it is."

We finished the food, and I tossed all the trash, sitting against the headboard of the bed with my feet propped up. My boots were unlaced and ready for me to step in, left on the floor within easy reach. I had already placed my gun on the bedside table. While she slept, I would clean it, but not until then.

"There's only one bed." She bit her lip.

"Yeah. That's all that was left." Shit. I didn't think about how that might look to her. "I know you needed rest, so I took it. Don't worry. I won't be sleeping."

She arched a brow. "You're not going to sleep?"

"No. I can't keep you safe if I'm not awake."

"Talon."

"Yeah, beautiful?"

"You can't stay awake all night."

"I won't invade your space." Leaning over, I pulled down the blanket, gesturing for her to lay down. "Get some rest. We're not leaving until dark. I paid up the room for two nights."

"My sleep schedule is off." She yawned. "I hate that."

"We'll fix it later."

She pulled the blanket up to her chin, resting her cheek on the pillow as she faced me. "Do you think they'll find us?"

"No," I replied firmly, hoping to alleviate her fear. "And if they do, I have friends I can call to help us. They aren't far."

"I don't know why I trust you," she blurted, biting her lip afterward. "You could hurt me as soon as I close my eyes."

"Do you think I would do that?"

"No, and that's weird. I know you won't." Her eyes closed as she sighed. "I don't have the energy."

"To what?" I asked, fighting the instinct to pull her close and hold her while she slept.

"Hmmm?"

She was too tired to finish the thought.

"Night, beautiful. I'm here if you need me."

She didn't answer, but I knew she heard me when a smile lifted the corners of her lips.

I slid from the bed and moved across the room, knowing that if I didn't, I would end up crossing a line I couldn't return from.

Chapter 5

GAIL

"GAIL. GET UP, BABY. We've got company."

I jolted awake from my dreams, throwing the covers back as I sat up and rubbed the sleep from my eyes.

"Here. Get dressed. I already took everything else out."

He handed over my bra and panties, turning his head as I whipped off his t-shirt. Once I had my clothes on and shoes tied, I held out his shirt.

"You might as well wear it. It's too fucking hot out for my leather jacket, but this will keep you covered more than a tank top."

He was right about that. I pulled his shirt back over my head and shoved my arms through the sleeves.

My hair was a tangled mess, and I reached for it, quickly braiding the long strands together in one thick plait. When I reached the end, I pulled the hair tie off my wrist and secured the end of the braid.

Talon ticked his chin my way. "That's impressive."

"I learned to braid fast when I was a girl."

He reached for my hand and tugged my body close. "I need you to be quiet. No talking."

I nodded, staring up at him as he slipped the bike helmet on my head.

Talon buckled the strap and led me toward the motel door, slowing as he approached it. "I heard bikes rolling in about twenty minutes ago. It's not an ally club. Trust me when I say we need to leave as quietly and quickly as possible."

Shit.

He peeked out the window first, pausing to ensure no one had come around the back of the motel yet. His hand grasped mine, and he opened the door, rushing toward his bike.

I sat on the seat without a word, wrapping my arms around his stomach when he sat in front of me. He didn't start it right away, walking the bike closer to the road first. My heart rate picked up when I heard voices. It sounded like a party with music so loud it thumped my chest as I clutched Talon's shirt and bunched the material in my fingers.

His right hand lowered, briefly squeezing my thigh before returning to the handlebar. He tried to reassure me, but I knew nothing about bikers or how their clubs interacted. Everything I understood came from books or television.

The sun hovered above the horizon, too bright to conceal us from the gathering at the front of the motel. The engine roared to life, rumbling as we surged forward, picking up speed as we turned onto the road. The wind whipped around us and billowed my clothes against my skin. Talon seemed immune to its reach as his tight black shirt stayed molded to his skin as if carved from solid obsidian.

I glanced behind us only once, noting with relief that no one followed. The long stretch of Hwy 95 led us farther from the motel, and within minutes, we'd left danger far behind.

Talon never slowed; his pace relentless as his focus remained on the road.

It almost felt like he'd forgotten I still clenched my thighs around his body. When I wondered if he would pull over and talk to me or stop soon, his hand lowered, slowly gliding along my thigh until his palm reached my hip and squeezed.

That one simple act demolished any doubt I had that we shared a mutual attraction. He'd touched my face with a gentle caress. Twice. He insisted I wear his helmet. His gaze raked over me with intense heat whenever our eyes met. What did that mean?

Talon risked his life to keep me safe. Was it only duty? Did my brother, his president, order him to protect me with his life? Because that was how Talon acted, like my life was somehow more precious than his own.

Strange.

But what about the way he looked at me at the hotel? It wasn't indifferent. And no, it wasn't only attraction. He avoided the question when I asked, the same night he found me huddled on the floor and terrified, but I felt something more from him. Then. And definitely now.

A rumble of thunder rippled above our heads, and I looked up, catching the dark gray clouds rolling in from the east. Lightning struck next, flashing in a wide arc ahead of us, branching out with spindly fingers that torched a tree's limbs off to our right. Shit. This storm was moving fast.

We were right out in the open.

Another boom cracked across the sky, followed by more lightning. I jolted when the third strike exploded directly above our heads. A screech escaped as I hugged Talon's ribcage tighter.

He yelled something I couldn't hear above the wind.

And then. . .the sky opened. Rain fell in thick, heavy sheets that soaked our clothes within seconds. The only protection I had came from the helmet. Talon had nothing.

45

He kept shaking his head, trying to fling water from his face and away from his eyes. His visibility had to be slim. I worried we would crash. The visor protected my face from the rain, but I couldn't see a damn thing.

To top it off, I wore the wrong fucking clothes.

My long tank top and shorts clung to my body, plastered to my skin. The material kept inching up my legs to rub against my inner thighs. The third time I reached to tug them back down, Talon grasped my wrist with a noise that sounded like a growl. He brought my hands together, and I locked them together around his waist, trying not to squirm against his back.

Having his shirt on top of the tank only pressed more wet, cold cloth to my skin. I shivered, unable to stop the tremors in my body. Every exposed area grew colder, lashed by the wind until I winced from the pain.

When I entered my house after work the night of the break-in, I didn't notice the mess as I headed into my room. In the dark, I fumbled for the light and flipped it on, undressing as I walked toward my walk-in closet. I began tossing clothes into my laundry basket, already overheated from the long, grueling day.

Only when I left my bedroom did I become aware of my surroundings, taking in the mess as I stood there, shocked to find someone had entered my home and caused such destruction. And now I wore barely anything and didn't have a change of clothes either. This was a nightmare.

Talon gripped my arm, holding it against his chest. He shouted something about finding shelter, and I nodded. The road signs indicated the next rest stop was closed. No hotel vacancy for thirty miles. I wrapped my arms and legs tighter around Talon, and he pointed to the right.

With all the rain and my limited visibility, I didn't see shit.

I felt us go off-road as the bike jostled my bottom on the seat before coming to an abrupt stop. Talon shut down the engine and turned, scooping up my body as I wrapped my legs around his waist.

My hands slid up his shoulders and around his neck as I buried my face in the hollow of his throat.

Probably not a great idea in a bike helmet. I nearly smacked him on the chin.

Rain pelted us as he ran, holding me with one arm as he kicked with his boot and shoved with his empty hand. A door flew open and crashed, almost at the exact moment lightning lit up the sky. Thunder boomed, rattling the walls around us.

Talon unbuckled the strap beneath my chin and lifted the helmet, dropping it on the ground before his hands gripped the back of my thighs, keeping me in place. "You okay?"

He sounded anxious. . .and worried. Did bikers ever worry about anything?

I couldn't stop trembling enough to answer.

"Fuck. I've got a blanket in my saddlebags. I'll try not to get it wet." He set me down, rushing out of the structure he'd brought me into, and from what I could tell, we found a barn. An old, rickety barn with part of the roof missing. Water poured inside on the opposite side of where I stood, soaking a large pile of old hay and rusted farm tools.

I rubbed my arms as I shivered, too stiff to move.

Talon entered and slammed the door shut, latching the fraying rope attached to the handle onto a curved nail poking out from a nearby beam. He frowned as he approached, lifting the blanket and shaking his head.

"I need to get you warm. You're soaked." His gaze focused on my chest as I shivered, taking in my hard nipples as he blinked. He swallowed. Hard. "You need to strip."

"S-strip?" I asked, teeth chattering. "Like naked?"

He smirked. "Yeah, beautiful. We both need to lose the clothes fast."

He shrugged off his leather vest and draped it over a peg, dangling the blanket before me. "Come on. Don't be shy."

Sighing, I tugged on the hem of his shirt and managed to lift it over my head, followed by my tank top. It wasn't easy. My shorts clung to my thighs during the process, and I struggled with the material, growing flustered.

Warm hands rested on my hips. "Hey."

I met his gaze, startled by the soft blue of his eyes and the hunger he didn't hide. "I'm self-conscious," I admitted.

"About?"

"My legs. They're. . . big and flabby."

His eyes narrowed. "Who the fuck told you that?"

"Uh," I paused, trying not to tear up. "My stepdad, for one."

He brought my body closer, slowly moving his hands toward my inner thighs. "You see this?"

I nodded, biting my lip.

"Fucking beautiful. Sexy. So goddamn delicious I want a taste." He lowered his head, pressing a kiss to my chilled skin. "I'd gobble you up, baby, and enjoy every moment."

My eyes widened.

"So, don't ever," he rose to his full height, "*ever* tell me any part of your body isn't fucking amazing because you turn me on." To punctuate his point, he reached for my hand and held it to his crotch. . .and the massive erection tenting his wet jeans.

"Oh, God," I gasped, wrapping my hand around his thick shaft. "You're huge."

"And all yours, whenever you want me."

"You mean that?"

"I do."

"In this barn?"

He nodded.

"On your bike?"

He nodded again, adding a growl.

"I guess that means you like me," I grinned.

He rolled his hips, pressing his cock into my hand. "I don't just like you, Abigail Holmes. I fucking want you. In my bed. On my bike." He tapped his heart. "And right fucking here."

I blinked, pulling my hand away. "I don't know you, Talon. We just met."

Did I want to get to know him? Yes! Was I worried I'd be another woman in the long list he fucked and left behind? Yes.

He frowned. "Okay. I accept that. For you, it's only been two days. For me, it's been over two months. I already know everything I need to know about you, baby."

"Really?" I asked with a shiver. "Like what?"

"Hold on. We'll come back to that." Talon held up the blanket. "Take off the rest. We need to let those clothes air dry."

Five minutes later, I sat on an overturned crate, bundled in the blanket and naked underneath. Talon finished forming a bunch of rocks into a circle, tossing in pieces of dry wood and hay he'd found while searching the barn. He flicked his lighter and touched the flame inside the pit, igniting the dry kindling. The fire sparked to life, quickly consuming the hay but burning into the logs until the barn grew warm.

I finally began to thaw, no longer shivering as my fingers and toes relaxed. "You're good at this. I bet you were a boy scout."

He snorted. "Fuck no. I learned this shit from my sponsor when I prospected for the Devil's Murder."

"How old were you?"

"Eighteen."

Wow. "That's young."

"Not too young to know what I wanted out of life."

Fair enough.

Talon crouched in front of the fire, lifting his hands to test the heat. "It'll burn for a while. I've got plenty of logs to add to it. We'll have dry clothes in a few hours."

He already draped our things nearby. . .which left him in nothing but a pair of dark boxer briefs that hugged his muscular thighs.

I tried not to stare at his bare back or the dark ink spreading across his broad shoulders, covering every inch from his neck to his waist. A mural of fascinating artwork that included a giant crow perched on a hill of skulls, overlooking a graveyard. Several names were scrolled across the headstones, including Rook. For some reason, the name sounded familiar.

Talon turned and faced me, stretching as he rolled his shoulders and cracked his neck. My greedy gaze devoured the taut muscles and his chiseled, perfectly shaped abdominals before slipping lower, admiring the two V-shaped muscular grooves alongside his hips.

"See anything you like, beautiful?"

Shit. He caught my stare. I decided to be honest since I asked the same of him. "Yes."

His lips twitched at the corners. "Love that about you, baby. You're a breath of fresh air."

"Because I'm not a liar?"

"Well, yes, partially, but also because I find it fucking sexy that you keep your word, you're honest, hardworking, and you've got a killer smile."

I couldn't help blushing at his compliments.

"Get used to me saying those things. You need to hear them. Whatever fucked up shit your stepdad or anyone else said to you doesn't matter. It's not true."

"I appreciate you think so, Talon."

He shook his head, lowering to his knees in front of me.

"I've been watching you, Gail. I *see* you."

His palm cradled the side of my face as he leaned closer. "You're fucking beautiful, but that's not what makes my heart pound. It's you. *Everyfuckingthing* about you."

"You're good," I whispered, lifting my finger to trace the black raven's wings that stretched from his left shoulder, across his chest, and around his right shoulder. More black ink swirled above and up his neck, stopping underneath his jaw. My fingertips grazed the edge, pulling away but he reached out and snatched my hand, dropping a kiss on top.

"I don't have a problem waiting until you're ready."

"You act like us being together is a done deal."

A smile curved his lips. "Isn't it?"

Chapter 6

UNDERTAKER

T HE FUCKING DEVIL'S MURDER MC.

A rival club. My enemies.

They got too involved in my shit. Kept sticking their noses where they didn't belong.

And then they fucking killed my V.P. Chronos, followed by my S.A.A. Grudge. It didn't stop there. They took out over a dozen of my Dirty Death brothers, dwindling our numbers. My pack was at half-strength. Too fucking vulnerable now.

They were growing restless and losing sight of our goals. To help make it right, I needed to mate. I had to breed and secure my line. That would ease the burden my pack felt.

Fuck. "Sadie," I snarled, fumbling in the dark as all my senses heightened but one. My vision had been stolen. Snatched away by that fucking useless cocksucker Carson Phillips.

Ah, but not so useless, is he?

I ignored the inner voice of the vargulf.

My concentration narrowed to the hunt—Sadie's scent.

And *goddamn*, she smelled intoxicating.

There wasn't a place she could run that I wouldn't find her. Losing my sight slowed me down—a regrettable technicality. I didn't need it to follow the musk that originated between her thighs. Memories of her soft, silky skin and the floral aroma invaded my senses. I would find her, and I would take what I needed, with or without her consent. The last of my patience eroded.

I needed to fuck. I had to pin her down on all fours and plow into her from behind until my cock overflowed her pussy with my cum. The thought of fucking her, of spilling into her warm body, overtook my focus.

She would never escape. The vargulf and his needs were too strong, too demanding.

I shook my head, swinging it from side to side as I tried to separate my wishes, needs, desires, and focus from the beast that subdued my wolf. Impossible. The vargulf had consumed that part of me and left nothing behind long ago.

All that existed now. . .all that ever would. . .was the monster.

He was voracious.

Everything narrowed down to Sadie. The woman I would fuck, claim, and breed until she filled my den with offspring worthy of succeeding me and taking the throne. My time as president would be short-lived, as it had with every alpha of our pack. Our lineage rose to power, became consumed with it, and left our humanity behind in the pursuit of the vargulf's power.

Even now, his energy pulsed through every cell, finetuning me into the ruthless beast my pack depended on.

My body and my mind became a weapon or tool, whichever was needed, to ensure success. Tonight, I shifted into the wolf's form and used his skills to locate my mate.

Her fear tainted the air and combined with her arousal.

She tried to deny the truth, but her body never could. She wanted the wolf. She needed to be subdued and held down, fucked into submission, bitten, and claimed.

And when my teeth clamped down on her neck and broke the skin, she would become my property, my mate, and I would chain her to the fucking bed until my seed took root inside her.

She kept me waiting for hours, thinking she could run as her pathetic lover tried to help her flee. He had tenacity. I almost respected that but he would die for forcing blindness upon me.

Sadie's delicate floral scent tickled my nose as I paused, sniffing the air. The vargulf growled inside me. His need increased. We could both sense how close our prey was and how the chase had turned her on. My cock lengthened and prepared to enter her, dripping with pre-cum.

She was so close. . .right. . . *here*.

My body shifted instinctually, and the wolf receded, bones popping and breaking as I reached for Sadie. She screamed. The sound vibrated along my shaft, and I growled, pushing her to the ground. A struggle ensued, but she could never fight off an alpha, especially when he decided to mate.

I flipped her body, placing her on her stomach as she pushed back against me. Only the thin material of a dress and panties separated us. I ripped the fabric away, shredding it from her skin as my palms skated down her ribcage and hips before gripping her bare ass.

"Mine," I howled.

My head lowered, and I inhaled. Musk. Fertile. *Mate.*

And I lost control. My hand brushed her pussy, pleased to find her wet and ready. Without delay, my hips surged forward, and I plunged inside Sadie. Her cry of pain mixed with pleasure as I began to rock, snapping my hips in a brutal rhythm. Nothing about this was gentle.

It couldn't be. The vargulf didn't make love. He *fucked.*

Sadie reached between her legs, fighting to reach her clit. I smacked her hand out of the way, rolling my fingers over the sensitive bundle. She would come because I got her off, no other way, including her own hand.

I pinned her to the ground, holding her wrists as her palms rested on the soft earth, nails digging into the grass. My hips never stopped moving. I rutted into her, harder, faster.

Every slam of my hips rocked her forward as she moaned.

Good. I wanted her to enjoy this.

The vargulf grew excited. He wanted to shift. To change into his wolf form and fuck her like a beast.

I fought him, refusing to risk hurting Sadie. The vargulf's cock was much thicker, the base of his shaft twice the size of my own, and I was already huge by human male standards. I'd tear her apart if I allowed it.

The vargulf laughed inside my head. He wanted carnage. The blood. The viscera that would follow.

He would gobble it all and consume my mate.

No. NO. I would not allow it.

Pulling back, I left Sadie's warm body and turned her over, brushing the hair out of her eyes as my fingers caressed her face. I didn't have to see her to know how she must be staring at me. My head lowered, and I found her lips, applying pressure as I kissed the woman I had fallen for, despite the fact that no vargulf ever successfully mated for long.

Driven by the instinct to hunt and kill, the vargulf often killed his mate after a few pups were born. His patience never lasted longer than that.

He would not murder or consume my Sadie.

With a hard thrust, I entered her willing, wet cunt a second time. My tongue tangled with hers, riding her body as waves of pleasure took over. I held her wrists above her head, pinning them down to subdue her, but she didn't fight.

"Undertaker," she breathed. "Make me come."

I snapped my hips to hers, grunting as our bodies mashed together. Her more petite, delicate curves provided the softest cushion. I wanted to stay lost in her forever.

My fangs elongated as my orgasm closed in. I wanted to bury them in her neck when I filled her with my seed, claiming her in the tradition of my ancestors. Not the vargulf's whim.

A primitive howl burst from my lips.

I was so fucking close. I released one of her wrists, trailing my hand between us until I reached her swollen clit. She cried out as I applied pressure, circling and rubbing as she writhed beneath me. I felt it the moment she climaxed, clamping down on my cock. She came so hard that she released a gush of fluid, and I growled with triumph.

My mouth opened wide as my fangs grew another inch, aching to be buried in my mate. I lowered my head, finding her neck. I nuzzled her with my nose first, excited but also strangely humbled to finally connect to another soul in such an intimate way. I couldn't hold back any longer. My cock shot my load, filling her while I reached completion.

As my teeth closed around the delicate base of her throat, she screamed.

I thought it was pleasure. Fulfillment.

"Now!"

Something heavy crashed into the back of my skull as I felt the magic of the bond leave through my saliva and enter Sadie's body. Whatever trick she tried to pull would not prevent or stop the bond. We were one. Mated.

She was fucked and claimed. I had seeded her, noting with satisfaction that I could smell my cum, and it filled her womb.

I had to admit she was clever. I never suspected her betrayal. My Sadie was so much more than a pretty face and a perfect cunt. She proved it tonight.

A worthy adversary. The alpha's queen.

As I collapsed on top of her, I whispered the words in my heart and my head. Words she could never escape or deny.

"You're mine now, my mate."

I lost my grip on reality but knew when I awakened, I'd hunt. What a prize I had to chase.

I would kill the male who helped her and then fuck her again.

She would never escape me.

GAIL

A DONE DEAL.

THAT was what Talon meant. Together. Not just for one night, either.

God. The man was an endless flirt, but I *loved* it.

And the way he called me beautiful, using that husky, deep voice, made me want to jump him, say to hell with rules and waiting, and let him give me all the orgasms I could want.

But the logical, organized part of my brain insisted this was too soon, and I didn't know anything about Talon.

I stared into his summer sky-blue eyes and couldn't help cracking a smile. "Do you always go after what you want this relentlessly?"

He scoffed. "You think this is relentless?" He shook his head, a smirk riding his lips. "Baby, you haven't seen nothin' yet."

I believed him.

I shifted my bottom off the crate and found a comfortable spot on the ground, hugging the blanket tighter around my shoulders.

The heat in the room had dried the floor and pushed the moisture away from us. My gaze swept over the flames and returned to Talon.

"Ask me."

"Hmmm?"

"Ask me whatever you want to know. I'll tell you anything except club secrets. I can't risk my patch."

"Your patch?"

"This." He stood, picked up his leather vest, and took a seat beside me. "See this?" He indicated the logo on the back. "That's us. The Devil's Murder MC. My family."

I nodded, scanning the double pistons and black feathers.

He flipped the vest over. "This is a cut. It's the most important thing I own. My road name is on the front, and so is my rank. I'm an enforcer."

My fingers traced the patches that read TALON and ENFORCER on the front of the cut. "You earned this, didn't you? Like the military."

He snorted. "Not quite. We're on two sides of the law, beautiful. I prefer to make my own rules and follow the ones designated by my club. I answer to my pres, V.P., and my Sergeant at Arms. That's it."

"I see."

"But to answer your question, yes. I earned my patch and my spot in the club. I prospected for over a year first and got the shit beat out of me more than once." He laughed as his shoulders lifted in a shrug. "It made me tough."

"It sounds like a hard life," I observed.

"It can be," he admitted, "but here's the thing. You never go through it alone. The men in my club are family. Brothers. Closer than blood and far more trustworthy. I owe them my life, especially Rook and Crow."

"Who are they?"

"To answer that question, I have to explain something first."

"Okay."

"My old man was a workaholic. He stayed out late and wasn't around on the weekends. I suspected he was having an affair long before my mom figured it out."

"Oh, wow."

"When I confronted him about it, he laughed and told me to man up, get my dick wet, and leave him alone."

"What?" I asked, furious for Talon. "What an asshole. Sorry."

"Don't be sorry, baby. You're right. He was a shitty father. Everything I learned about being a man came from Raven. He was my sponsor and a damn good one."

"He's the one who took you camping?"

"And fishing, not to mention he took me under his wing and taught me the basics about auto repair. He's like a father to me. So was Rook. I wouldn't be here if it weren't for them."

"I think there's more to this story."

"Yeah, there is. I won't drag it out, but I got wild. Booze. Cigarettes. Parties. Girls." He cleared his throat. "And one night, I took it too far."

"Uh-oh."

"I got in a fight at a bar and pulled a knife." He shook his head as I sucked in a breath. "I cut a man's arm and threatened to slit his throat. All because I didn't want to look weak or be a disappointment to my old man. He wasn't even there, and he still had a way of poisoning me."

My hand rested over the fist he clenched on his lap. "Go on."

"I got thrown in county lock up and called my dad to bail me out."

His gaze cut across the room, lost in the memory.

"He decided to humiliate me to teach me a lesson. He yelled and called me every name he could think of. Ranted for over fifteen minutes before anyone told him to shut up. You'll never guess who did."

I already figured it out. "Rook."

His head turned, and he smiled. "Smart. Yeah, Rook and Crow were in that jail cell, too. My father had no idea when he walked away. He turned his back on me and set me free at the same time."

"Wow," I said a second time. "That's crazy."

"It doesn't end there. Turned out my father and another member of the club were cousins. They grew up together but lost touch and went their separate ways after my father refused to have anything to do with the club."

"Rook? Or Raven?"

"You have a hell of an intuition, beautiful." He slid his arm around my shoulders and tucked my body against his side. "Raven is my uncle."

"That's so awesome. You found family."

"In more ways than one. I never looked back."

"And Rook and Crow?"

"My old pres and my new pres. Father and son. That's how the Devil's Murder has been run for decades."

That made sense. "Where are your parents now?"

He dropped a kiss on top of my head before he answered. "My father died a few years back from lung cancer."

"I'm sorry, Talon."

"It's sad, but I don't dwell on it."

"I can understand why."

"My mom lives in Henderson. I visit her all the time."

"That's sweet."

He shifted, tilting my chin up until our eyes met. "I need to kiss you. It's burning something awful inside me."

"What is?" I asked with a whisper.

"Carrying this overwhelming, intense feeling for you. It's like I can't breathe unless we're touching. I'm fucking turned on too."

I couldn't help glancing at his crotch. *Yep. Massive erection detected.*

"Never felt coiled this tight about any woman before now," he admitted. "I want to fuck, make love, eat your delicious pussy, fuck again, and have you ride me. Then, start the process again until the fog in my head clears. I don't think it will, though," he rasped, not hiding the hunger in his eyes. "You're fucking naked under that blanket, and I'm so horny at the thought I'm surprised I can fucking talk."

"Talon?"

"Yeah, baby?"

I let the blanket fall open, uncovering my body. "Touch me."

Chapter 7

TALON

"TOUCH ME."

THOSE TWO words seared my brain, and all thought fled, replaced by feral need, lust, and the all-consuming desire to claim this woman for my own. I had her on her back, settling between her luscious thighs in less than a heartbeat.

"Tell me to back off if this isn't what you want, Gail. This is your only chance. I swear to fuck I won't be angry with you. I'll understand."

Please tell me that you want me with the same intensity.

"I can't," she admitted, biting her lower lip. "I want you, Talon. And I don't want to fight it."

Fuck. Yes.

My body reacted before my mind caught up.

Hooking under her knees, I tugged her hips forward, lifting her off the ground and burying my face between her legs.

All I imagined for two months was the way she tasted.

Fuck. It was worth the wait. Her unique flavor was better than I ever could have conjured in my head. She drove me wild with the first swipe of my tongue through her soft folds. With one hand, I caressed her belly while I licked at her soft center. Long, slow, purposeful licks until I grazed her clit with my thumb, teasing her before I speared my tongue inside her.

"Oh. God. Talon, *yes.*"

And now I really wanted to dig in and feast. My fingers slowly began rubbing the hood of her clit, moving in tight circles, and then I used my mouth, sucking until her hips bucked. I held her in place, lashing my tongue through her slick folds and enjoying every fucking second.

Her moans. Fuck. Those sounds she made. *Addicting.*

My gaze traveled up the length of her body, taking in her slightly rounded belly and generous breasts. *She's fucking stunning.* Her knees wobbled and then fell apart wider, inviting me to press closer against her. I groaned when her fingers speared through my hair and gripped tight, forcing my head into her cunt. She rode my face without a care, rolling her hips as soft cries left her mouth.

I had fought denial so long that now I had no barrier against it, not even when I realized I didn't have a condom. I slid two fingers inside her, curling upward, and working her clit until I felt her channel tighten around them.

"That's it, baby. Come for me."

A wail tumbled from her lips as her inner walls spasmed, and I placed my mouth on her pussy, licking at the wetness that escaped. Gail jolted as her thighs quivered.

Hell yeah.

Nothing stroked a guy's ego like a woman's legs shaking during and after her orgasm.

She sighed with contentment when I kissed a pathway up her body, running my tongue over her soft stomach, stopping to focus on the mounds that seemed made for me as they fit into my palm. Just enough overflow to be a tease.

"These tits, babe," I growled. "Fuck. I love them."

My tongue circled her left nipple, and I licked at her skin, loving the fresh, sweet taste of her on my tongue. I nibbled and sucked, bringing the buds to tight peaks. She arched her back and moaned.

With open-mouthed kisses, I continued upward, sucking on her neck and, finally, pausing to stare into her eyes. She'd have a choice about what happened next. "I don't have a condom."

"Oh, Talon," she moaned, writhing underneath me as my body covered hers, rolling her hips as my cock nudged between her thighs, almost lodging inside from her desperate movements.

"We can pick this up later, beautiful. I'll look forward to it."

Indecision crossed her delicate features, and I knew we needed to wait. I didn't like it, and neither did my cock, but I also wouldn't fuck her just because my body demanded it.

"You would stop if I asked," she murmured with awe. "God, Talon. That's all I need to know. You respect me."

"Of course," I began, groaning when she pushed me onto my back. Her hips straddled mine as she brushed her pussy against the edge of my shaft. My dick slid through her folds. *So wet. So warm.*

"I want to ride you."

She grasped my cock, lifted up to let the tip brush her pussy, and impaled herself on me, taking me into her body in one swift, mind-blowing, downward thrust.

I. Fucking. Saw. Stars.

She snapped her hips, unafraid to find a pace and rhythm she liked. She rode me with abandon, taking what she needed.

Sexy as fuck.

Goddamn.

I'm in love.

A soft cry escaped Gail's lips as I rolled my hips, lifting off the ground to go deeper, sweeter, hitting that perfect angle. I held her hip with one hand and strummed her clit with the other. Fuck. I needed her to enjoy this as much as I was because this wasn't a one-time deal. No, I had to ensure she was mine and I would use my dick if it helped. *Every damn time.*

"You feel so fucking good," I groaned.

"Talon. You're so deep it's like I feel you everywhere."

My hands shifted to her ass, tugging her into me as our bodies met again and again. The storm raged around us, pelting the barn with heavy rain and wind. Neither of us paid attention to it, too far lost in our own storm.

"Harder, faster, Talon."

Anything you want, baby. My body tightened, and my thrusts grew erratic. Fuck. I needed her closer.

Somehow, I managed to sit up, staying deep inside her. My right arm curled around her back, hooking her shoulder and pulling her into every thrust. Waves of pleasure built to the point that I knew I wouldn't be able to last much longer.

"Talon! I'm coming!"

Fuck. *Yeah, she is.* I wanted to see that expression on her face every fucking night. Blissed out. Lost in me and what we shared.

"Perfect," I murmured, loving that she became so limp she could hardly rock back against me, taking my dick like a good girl.

My restraint snapped. No more measured or precise strokes. No holding back. I was too gone. A growl rumbled up my chest as I drove up into her, wildly pumping my hips. With a shout, I let go and shuddered, coming so fucking hard that I fought to catch my breath.

My chest heaved as my forehead rested against Gail's.

"That was amazing," she whispered as I caught her heart-stopping smile.

"Hell yeah," I agreed, brushing my lips over her sweet mouth as I locked her against my chest. "So fucking good."

I slipped from her body and rested against the blanket, wrapping my arms around her and refusing to sever the connection.

Seeing my mate so relaxed and contented sent a buzz of soothing energy through my body.

I felt her emotions. Her happiness and affection. The completeness that fulfilled her.

Mate. The word swirled in my head. My mind awakened as the thought lit up my brain.

Not just a soul mate. No ordinary bond. This surpassed both.

A mate. The forever mate of a crow.

My goddess. My curvy dream girl.

I didn't even know how badly I craved a mate until I saw Gail.

My brain fired in all directions, consumed with the knowledge unlocked in my head. I had considered this often for the last two months, but now that I had confirmation and felt the bond snap into place, I dismissed all doubt.

My crow knew exactly where his mate had been.

Caw...caw.

The crow's ebony wings spread outward above us, sensing the connection I just formed. He chittered in the sky, squawking out a raspy, celebratory kraa. I could see him through the gaps in the roof where the wood had rotted.

I dozed for several hours and held Gail as she slept. When the storm subsided, I woke her, watching as she dressed. I gave her a bottle of water and a protein bar from my bag.

"Be right back. I need to check in with Crow. We'll head to the safe house next."

She nodded, chewing as her gaze focused on the bright blue sky and beams of sunshine through the cracks in the barn.

I walked outdoors, sliding on my shades after I pulled them from my cut.

"Where the fuck is my sister?" Crow asked when he answered my call, his tone proving I waited too long to get in touch because he sounded *pissed*.

"Safe. We're headed toward Tonopah. We got caught in a storm and had to take shelter, but no one has followed us."

"You sure about that?"

"Positive, pres."

"You going to the house with the pool and that huge deck?"

"Yeah. It's perfect." Secluded. Pretty. Off the highway and away from trouble.

"I'm sending Cuckoo to meet up with you. Anything you need, he'll get it."

"Appreciate it, pres."

"I spoke to Grim. Get Abigail to The Crossroads if there's trouble."

"Will do," I promised.

"Is she okay after all this shit? Not freaking out?"

"Yeah, she is. She's like her brother. Tough."

He grunted. "Check in when you're settled. Cuckoo will be there by noon."

"No worries, pres. I got this."

"I know."

After the call, I walked inside the barn and held out my hand. "Come on, beautiful. Let's get on the road."

Gail laced our fingers. "I'm with you, Talon."

Those words settled the anxiety in my gut. I hated being vulnerable on the road with her on the back of my bike and the chance that the club's enemies could be waiting to ambush us. But she trusted me. I wouldn't let her down.

GAIL BEGAN TAPPING MY thigh like a madwoman about thirty minutes after we left the barn. I glanced over my shoulder at her but didn't have a clue what got her so excited until I noticed the sign on the road. In-N-Out Burger.

I took the next exit and pulled to a stop at a light. My hand moved to her thigh, and I caressed the soft skin, brushing my fingers back and forth. I didn't think I'd ever be able to get enough of her. Remembering how we spent the time during the storm in that barn awakened my dick, and lust surged through my brain. If I could find a place to take her and dive between her thighs again, I'd do it. Right now.

Once the light flipped to green, we rode to the restaurant, and I parked my bike, rising off the seat. Gail hung the helmet and turned toward me, pressing a hand into her stomach. I heard the loud rumble as I snickered.

"I guess I wore you out, huh? Need fuel, baby?"

She moved closer, eliminating the space between our bodies. "If you're going to make me come that hard, I need food afterward."

Done.

I clasped our hands and nearly dragged her inside, grinning when she ordered enough food for two people on her own. I added what I wanted and paid the bill, watching her fill a large cup with unsweetened tea.

Shaking my head, I joined her, filling my cup full of sugary soda and not ashamed of it.

When our number was called, I reached for the bags and strode out the door, pushing back on the glass to hold it open for her. My mother beat that shit into my head when I was a boy. If a woman didn't want the door held open for her, she'd tell me. Otherwise, you fucking do it every time.

"Do we have time to sit at one of the tables and eat?"

The place was busy, but I didn't see the harm in it. I doubted anyone knew who the fuck we were, and they didn't look long when they spotted my cut or club colors.

"Sure."

We sat at a table with a bright-colored umbrella, shielded from the sun, and talked for over an hour. We discussed all kinds of shit. Nothing. Everything. It wasn't the specific conversation, just the moment we had together, showing me I could have something real with this woman—a little slice of heaven in the middle of hell.

Life wasn't easy for me or my club. We had to claw our way to get to where we were. Lots of sacrifice along the way. I wouldn't change a thing about patching into the Devil's Murder, but I sure loved sitting across from Gail and watching her smile.

I probably wouldn't remember everything we said later, but I knew I'd never forget how beautiful she looked or how I already decided that I needed to marry her. She wouldn't just be my ol' lady. I wanted her for my wife, too. My forever.

My crow cawed from nearby. *Yeah. I know. Take it slow.*

He didn't want to scare or overwhelm Gail. I didn't either.

After we finished eating, we rode to the safe house. I emptied my saddlebags after parking my bike and led her to the house.

Outside the door, she paused, leaning against the stucco exterior. "This was the perfect date, you know."

Date? I blinked at her, not quite getting it.

Gail pushed off and lifted a hand, sliding it around my neck. I almost melted from the heat of her touch. She lightly scratched the back of my neck with her nails, and I nearly moaned. Fuck. What was she sayin' again?

"We rode on your Harley and ate at my favorite restaurant. That's a perfect date," she explained.

Hell yeah.

"Better than any date you've ever had?" Or the dumb fucks she dated recently?

"No comparison."

I fucking grinned so damn wide. "Do I get a kiss at the end of our first date?"

"You do." She pressed her mouth to mine, and I groaned.

So fucking sweet and soft and addicting.

When she nibbled on my bottom lip and sucked it into her mouth, I almost lost control.

"Beautiful," I growled as we separated, "that's the kind of kiss you give a man when you want forever."

"I'll remember that."

She didn't reject the idea. That made me so fucking happy.

"Let's get inside. It's cold."

Chapter 8

TALON

Two weeks later

I SPOILED GAIL AS soon as I got the chance. She lit up when I opened my laptop, gave her my login and credit card information, and told her to shop. So. . .she shopped.

My woman bought enough clothes, shoes, toiletry items, undergarments, and everything else that she needed to supply a small army. To be fair, she had to leave it all behind when we rushed from her house. Cuckoo delivered packages almost daily. He wasn't my first choice, but Crow insisted.

I waited for him on the back deck of the ranch-style house the club bought a few years back, smoking since I didn't have shit to do but wait. The architecture included an open floor plan and large windows, a U-shape, and a lower-pitched roof. We included a finished basement and a panic room. All the safe houses had an armory inside with enough guns and ammo to take a stand if we needed.

The rumble of his bike alerted me to his presence before he appeared. And fuck. . .he couldn't dress normally and try to blend in. I scrubbed a hand down my face when I saw his costume.

Cuckoo rolled his bike to a stop and cut off the engine. He turned my way, wearing a bright green dragon costume with shiny gold, pink, and purple scales. The top stretched over his head as the mouth opened, revealing pointed white teeth made from felt.

For fuck's sake.

He looked ridiculous. Scales poked out all the way down his back. The ones beneath his cut puffed out the leather and made him look like a deformed, hunchback dragon.

I didn't bother asking him why he chose this costume. Cuckoo always had a reason, and I didn't want the headache when he gave the explanation.

"What are you, Puff the Magic Dragon?" I asked, shaking my head. Then I spotted the tail. "You rode your fucking bike with that tail?"

Cuckoo winked. "You bet I did. All I had to do was fold it a bit and sit on it. Didn't get stuck in the tires either. So Carrion can fuck right off."

"You know he told you that so you wouldn't crash, right?"

Carrion saw things. His crow had visions, and while that freaked us out more than a few times, he never got shit wrong.

The gift manifested after Carrion died. Falcon, the club's healer, brought him back, but he wasn't the same afterward. There was darkness inside him, and he often stuck to the shadows like they had become home.

For some reason, Cuckoo liked to fuck with him. Fucking idiotic if you asked me. Carrion could sometimes see the future, which meant he had the ability to play a reaper. Not that he ever decided anyone else's fate. He handed over information and walked away, disappearing from the chaos he always left behind.

Cuckoo sucked on his teeth and then frowned. "Fuck. He tricked me."

"Or he saved you," I pointed out.

"I'm gonna kick his ass."

"You wanted to crash?" I scrubbed a hand down my face. "Did you bring the packages?"

"Yeah, they're in my saddlebags."

I noticed he didn't answer me about wanting to crash his bike. *Crazy fucker.*

Cuckoo handed over several padded envelopes and a box, following me inside as his tail swished behind him. We didn't send anything to the safe house address. Too risky.

"Hey, Cuckoo," Gail greeted as he entered. She blinked.

Yeah, babe. He's wearing a dragon costume.

"Hey, Gail. What're you makin'?"

She fed him every time he showed up.

"Nothing special. Spaghetti and meatballs. All homemade, though. Garlic bread and salad, too. You want some?"

"Fuck yeah, I do." He sat at the counter, flopping onto a stool as he pushed the dragon's head backward, folding a few of the scales that protruded down his back. "I'm starving."

"You should eat before you ride for so long."

The trip was a little under three and a half hours. Cuckoo could do that without any problem, but he didn't tell Gail. Hell, that was hardly any time at all in the saddle for any of us. Bikers took long rides on the regular. Our club organized runs even when we didn't have shit to take care of. It kept us sharp.

"And not be hungry for your cookin'? Hell no."

She gave him a sweet smile for the compliment.

I dropped the packages in the living room and walked to the fridge, pulling out a couple of beers and sliding one across the countertop. Cuckoo picked it up and popped the top, guzzling half the bottle before he belched.

I thumped the back of his head. "Watch your fuckin' manners, asshole."

He grinned. "You're so sensitive, honey."

I flipped him off.

Gail snickered. "You fight like an old married couple."

She wasn't wrong. Cuckoo had that effect on most of us. He liked to shake things up, and he was fucking good at it.

Gail served a heaping plate to Cuckoo and then placed one in front of me. I got a kiss on the cheek. Cuckoo didn't.

She joined us, sitting on a stool I placed to my left. "So. I was wondering if you could tell me why there are always crows around here."

Cuckoo paused with his fork halfway to his mouth.

I swallowed the bite I had in mine.

Neither of us spoke.

"It just seems odd," she continued, "because I hear cawing often. It's like they're watching over us. Isn't that strange?"

Cuckoo lowered his head and shoveled food into his mouth, avoiding the topic by ignoring her words and chewing his bites so long they were probably mush.

"Well, we're friendly with them," I replied.

Cuckoo snorted.

I shot him a glare.

"Friendly? What does that mean? Do you feed them?"

"Sure," Cuckoo chuckled.

I punched his shoulder.

She took a bite of her salad, thinking it over. "Aren't crows supposed to be good luck?"

"They are," I replied, giving her a tight smile. "This is fucking delicious, beautiful. I'm fucking lucky you spoil me."

Her expression softened. "You spoil me, too."

Damn right, I did.

Cuckoo finished his food and stood. "Gotta run. Thanks, Gail." He walked over and pecked her cheek. "You're a fucking keeper."

She laughed, and I narrowed my eyes.

"Don't worry, Talon. I won't try to steal her away."

"Fuck off," I laughed as he left, swishing that fucking dragon tail behind him.

GAIL

I HAD QUESTIONS. *A lot* of questions.

I gave Talon two weeks, but now I felt restless and anxious, and I worried about my home, my car, and the dead body inside my bedroom. Nothing had been communicated to me, almost as if my brother had ordered Talon to remain silent and keep me sheltered. Ridiculous. I was a part of this now. I became involved the night my house was broken into and everything trashed.

No reason for secrets now.

Talon noticed my frustration as I cleared the counter and rinsed off the dishes after Cuckoo left. I left them in the sink, pulling down a bottle of Jack from the cupboards and placing a shot glass on the coffee table in the front room as I parked my ass on the black leather sofa.

"Talk to me, beautiful."

Talon sat across from me, leaning forward as his elbows rested on his knees.

I had so many things I wanted to ask I hardly knew where to start. "Where is my brother?" I asked, pouring a shot.

"At The Roost. Our clubhouse."

"Where's that?" I lifted the drink and tossed it down my throat, hissing at the burn that followed.

"In Henderson."

"Why hasn't he come yet?" I poured another shot, holding the drink as I stared into his eyes. "Answer me."

"I don't know," he replied.

I drank the shot, quickly pouring another. "You're going to have to do better than that."

He frowned. "What's that going to accomplish?" He gestured to the bottle.

"Not much, but I'll feel less stabby."

He smirked. "You're that frustrated?"

"Yes," I growled, flinging back the liquor.

"Gail. Crow doesn't want to overwhelm you."

"Really?" I asked, not believing him. It wasn't that Talon lied. He didn't. I just couldn't wrap my head around the fact that my brother didn't care enough to join me right away. He sent one of his guys instead.

"Baby," he began.

"Don't call me that right now."

"Fine." He scrubbed a hand down his face. "We can talk about this."

"You're not the person I want to talk to right now. I. Want. My. Brother."

Yes. I sounded like a spoiled brat. It wasn't my usual way of handling things, but I was already overwhelmed.

Crow's absence made things worse, not better.

"I see," he replied, sitting back against the leather cushions.

The living room had been arranged so that the leather couches faced one another, one backed against a wall. Open floor plan leading into the dining room on the right. Large windows on the left. The coffee table stood between us on top of a dark gray rug. Almost all the flooring was hardwood throughout.

"Call him. Right now."

Talon sighed but pulled his phone from his cut.

"Wait."

He arched a brow.

"What's Crow's real name?"

"Austin."

"Okay. Call him and put it on speaker."

The line rang twice before a deep, gruff voice answered. "Is Abigail—"

"Austin," I blurted, cutting him off.

"Hey," he replied, his voice softening.

My heart pounded so hard I felt it in my throat. "Hi."

"I think I know why you're calling. I'm almost there. I'll see you in about an hour, maybe sooner."

He was already on his way. Wow.

"Okay."

"Abigail?"

"Yes?" I asked, hating that my throat felt tight with unshed tears.

"I didn't stay away because I didn't want to see you. I was hunting the men that are after you. Okay?"

"Okay," I repeated a second time.

"Let me talk to Talon."

"You're on speaker."

"We got shit to discuss, brother. Raven, Hawk, and Carrion are with me. Be ready."

"I hear you, pres."

The call ended.

My gaze flicked to Talon. "What did he mean? Be ready?"

"I don't know, but it's a universal warning to be ready for anything to go down. Stay sharp. Arm up. Watch our surroundings. And protect you with my life."

"All that from two words?"

His lips twitched with the beginning of a smile. "Yeah, babe. It's that simple."

I paced for the entire hour and drank two more shots. I had a good buzz going, which is the only reason I wasn't more nervous.

When the rumble of bikes alerted us of their arrival, I rushed to the window, eager to get a look at my brother. The only blood-related family I had.

The first thing that stood out was his height. He was taller than Talon, who was six foot four. Crow had impossibly broad shoulders and thick dark hair the same shade as mine. I noticed as soon as he lifted his helmet.

Power seemed to ooze from him as he turned and walked toward the front door with long, energetic strides.

I didn't see his face yet. His presence held me spellbound before he set foot inside.

"Yeah," Talon whispered next to me. "Crow has always been like that."

I wiped my sweaty palms off on my jeans.

A heartbeat later, Crow entered, striding toward me and coming to a halt a few feet from where I stood.

"Abigail."

"Gail," I whispered, staring at him in wonder. "I like to be called Gail."

"Gail," he acknowledged.

"I've seen you before."

He blinked. "You have?"

"Yes. I've got a picture." I walked to my purse and pulled out my wallet, removing the picture I'd held onto and never understood its importance. Until now. "This is my Uncle Derek—"

"That's me and my dad—"

Woah.

We locked eyes.

"That's my father. Austin Derek Holmes, Sr."

"But he's my Uncle Derek," I whispered. "He used to come and see me every other weekend. We went to the zoo."

My legs wobbled, and two sets of arms shot out.

Crow glared at Talon as he led me to the couch. I sat, too numb to speak.

"That must have been his way of keeping you safe."

"Why?" I asked, gutted by the fact that my father never wanted me to know his real identity. Tears filled my eyes, and I hated crying. I couldn't help it.

"Hey," Crow choked, "none of that."

A few tears slipped down my cheeks.

"Come here." He reached for me, and I didn't hesitate to wrap my arms around him, sniffling as he cleared his throat and hugged me back. "I'm sorry, Gail. I didn't know about you. I never did."

"What's this picture then?" I asked.

"I've never seen it."

"You haven't?"

"No. But it's me, my dad, I mean *our* dad, and a little girl I assume is you."

"It's one of my happiest childhood memories. I thought you were a friend from school. We went to the zoo that day, and Uncle Derek bought me a stuffed elephant because I told him how much I loved it. We had ice cream. I knocked yours out of your hand. You don't remember?"

Crow frowned. "No. I wish I did."

"I thought my dad died when I was a baby."

"He must have believed you were in danger to hide the truth from both of us. It's the only conclusion that makes sense."

"He hid the truth from everyone, Gail. I'm sorry," a gruff voice added.

I looked up, noticing the other men in the room for the first time. The one who spoke, an older guy with a graying beard and bald head, gave me an apologetic smile.

"I'm Raven. The V.P. of the Devil's Murder. Rook was my best friend."

Rook. Uncle Derek. My father. So many identities for the same man.

"You're Talon's uncle."

"Yes. That's Hawk." He pointed to the guy with all the piercings and facial tattoos. "And that's Carrion."

The last guy dressed all in black. He stayed quiet and hovered on the edge of the room as if he felt more at home in the shadows as night descended and the room darkened.

"Hi," I responded awkwardly to Hawk and then Carrion.

Hawk ticked his chin my way in greeting.

Carrion pushed off the wall and walked toward me, dropping to his knees so close we touched. How odd.

"You were a secret because he loved you so much."

I blinked. "How do you know that?"

Carrion's eyes rolled back, going white as I stared, shocked when his head snapped back and then forward when his eyes opened. "Rook left you something. It's at The Roost. You have to be the one to find it."

"Uh, okay."

Carrion turned to Crow. "Leave in the next thirty minutes. Delay any longer, and you won't reach The Roost in time." He stood, gesturing to Hawk. "We need to ride. Now."

Crow waved them off. "Go."

He didn't ask how Carrion knew any of this.

I stared at his retreating back and watched Hawk follow him out. "I'm scared." Fear had latched onto me with Carrion's words.

"That wasn't his intention," Talon promised.

Crow grimaced. "Carrion's a bit cryptic, but he told you those things because that's his gift. He likes to help."

"I'm so confused. None of this makes any sense." My logical brain kept trying to put all this information together in a neat, composed pile, and it wasn't working.

Outside, I heard multiple crows. The caws overlapped as if they were agitated or angry.

"The crows," I began as my brother rushed to his feet.

He glanced at his watch. "Ten minutes." He glanced at Raven, then Talon. "Carrion gave us thirty, but I'm not pushing it. Help her pack."

"Austin?" I asked as my voice cracked.

"You're riding with me, Gail. I won't let anything happen to you. I swear it."

I had to trust him.

With a nod, I placed the photo back in my purse and stood, rushing toward the room I used for the last couple of weeks. The same room I shared with Talon.

We didn't have sex again, but he held me every single night. And I lost my heart to him a little more with every day we spent together.

He reached for my hand and led me inside. "I'll grab a couple of bags. Pack what you can, and we'll send a prospect back for the rest."

Raven helped me as I emptied drawers and packed all the essentials. He cleared everything from the bathroom and placed it in my travel bag while Talon packed his own.

We were ready in six minutes.

Talon tilted my chin up as Raven grabbed a bag. "I don't know when I'll get a chance to do this again." His mouth covered mine, and the kiss that followed almost buckled my knees. He nibbled and licked at my mouth and groaned as we separated.

"Crow won't be happy," Raven announced.

"Not his choice," Talon responded, "it's hers."

Raven shook his head with a chuckle. "This should be fun."

Talon shrugged. "It'll work out."

I wanted to believe him, but when we exited the room, and Crow glanced at our clasped hands, he narrowed his eyes.

Yeah, Crow wasn't going to like this at all.

Chapter 9

GAIL

I STILL HAD WAY too many unanswered questions.

Crow insisted that I ride with him on the back of his bike, and with every mile on the road, I thought of something else to ask him. It was weird to ride with my brother instead of Talon. It felt off. Almost wrong.

I kept glancing behind me, trying to see Talon, but it was impossible with the helmet. Raven blocked him any way. Talon stayed in the last position, and I wondered what he would do when we arrived at our next destination. No one thought to mention where that would be or what I should expect. I was a detail-oriented girl. It bugged me.

After an hour and a half on the road, Crow took an exit. We rumbled through a nothing of a town with a sign that read Tonopah. The only thing that caught my attention was the creepy clown motel. You couldn't pay me enough to stay there.

I wasn't a fan of clowns.

On the outskirts of Tonopah, we approached a gated piece of land. When Crow pulled up, the prospect opened the gate and ushered us inside. We parked, and I stood, relieved to have my ass off that seat. My butt was sore, and I had to pee.

I unbuckled the helmet, lifted it over my head, and handed it to Crow. I wasn't sure what to call him. He never said. I figured if other bikers were around, I should use Crow. When we talked alone, I would use Austin.

I shook out my hair and turned, taking in the massive compound spread across the desert. A sign read The Crossroads on a door next to a covered patio with picnic tables. Another sign read Reaper's Custom Rides & Repairs above open bays where I could see men working on cars and motorcycles.

"Where are we?"

"The home of the Royal Bastards MC. The Tonopah, NV Chapter," Crow answered. "Come on. We're not sticking around out here."

"Good," Talon added.

He slipped an arm around my waist, and I could swear a hostile vibe radiated from him.

"You okay?"

He lowered his head close to my ear. "Yeah. Stay close to me."

I tugged on my bottom lip with my teeth. His response made me feel anxious. "Should I be worried?"

"No, beautiful. I just don't want to have to kick anyone's ass tonight."

"Why would you need to do that?"

He growled as we entered, not bothering to answer, and I felt eyes on all of us, especially me. Talon's grip tightened.

"Crow!" A deep voice boomed in greeting. "How the fuck are you, brother?"

Crow laughed, giving the big biker who approached him a slap on the back as they hugged. "I'll be better when I get my sister to The Roost."

The biker's eyes widened. "Your sister?" His gaze shot to me. "She sure looks like a Holmes."

Crow slid an arm around my shoulders and pulled me away from Talon. "Gail, meet Grim. He's the president of this rowdy bunch of bastards."

The room erupted in laughter and a few obscene jokes.

"Hi, Grim."

"Honey, this tall, crazy asshole and I go way back." Grim slightly slurred his words.

I couldn't hold back a smile. "I see."

He flung out an arm. "This is your home away from home. Eat, sleep, fuck, drink. Welcome to The Crossroads."

"Where every decision is probably a bad one," Crow joked.

Grim chuckled, leading Crow toward the bar.

I laughed as my brother stumbled into him. I'd never been in a biker club or a bar like this, and I spun in a slow circle, taking it all in, from the pool tables to the dark décor to the neon lights boasting the beers on tap. One sign made me giggle. A naked woman rode a reaper on a bike.

There were bikers everywhere. Women draped over most of them. Some wore next to nothing. I spotted a couch where a few had gathered who didn't look as skanky as the ones closer to the bar. I wondered how they fit in.

Talon's hand slipped into mine and led me across the room. We stopped at a deserted brown leather couch. He sat and pulled me onto his lap, tilting my chin down before he claimed my lips. His hands went to my ass and squeezed before his tongue pushed into my mouth. I circled his neck with my arms and leaned into him, enjoying the way he could devour me with something as simple as a kiss, when I heard a loud whistle.

In an instant, the bar quieted.

"Talon!" Crow roared.

"Yep, I knew that was coming," he muttered. "Yeah, pres?"

"Get your hands off my sister's ass!"

I dared to challenge my brother in front of everyone. "What if I want them there?"

Guffaws erupted around the room.

Crow turned red. "Move. Now," he ordered.

Talon slowly released me, and I pouted when my bottom landed on the couch.

Crow stalked across the bar, his expression thunderous.

Talon stood, ready to face whatever wrath awaited.

"What's happening?" I asked, concerned for both men.

"Well," Raven answered as he dropped next to me on the cushion, "I think your brother is feelin' protective over you and doesn't want anyone messing with his sister."

"It's not like that with Talon."

"Honey, I can see that, but your brother is kind of blind to it right now."

I didn't understand. What was the problem?

Crow reached us. Fury pulled his brows together as he snarled at Talon. "I gave you an order."

His voice was low and laced with venom.

"I understand that, pres. I tried."

"The fuck you did," he growled.

"Why don't we take this outside?" Raven asked as Crow got in Talon's face. "Or not."

"Why?" Crow's voice sounded strained. "I asked you not to touch her."

He did?

"My crow," Talon tried to explain, but he didn't get to finish.

"No. Don't you fucking say it."

"I won't lie to you, pres. The crow knows."

"No." He practically spit the word out. "Get the fuck out of here. Ride to The Roost. Now."

What?

I opened my mouth to object when Raven's hand reached for mine and squeezed it.

"This has to be worked out between them. It's not your place, honey."

"But it's about me," I argued.

"And they'll get to that when they cool off."

Talon gave a sharp nod to Crow. "I'm leavin', pres."

My brother's shoulders lost a little of their tension, but the anger didn't disappear from his face or the cold steel of his eyes.

Talon risked his wrath to turn to me. "I'll be waiting for you, beautiful." He tapped his heart. "You're right here."

God. This man. The way he made me feel. It was special. Intoxicating. Life-changing. "Talon."

"It's okay, baby. I'll see you tomorrow." He winked, nodded to Crow and Raven, and then strode to the door. He left without looking back.

My hand rose to my chest. "Raven?"

"Yeah, honey?"

"I'm hurting for both of them right now."

"I can see that. Trust me, it's gonna be fine."

Crow watched Talon leave and then marched to the bar, where a shot of whiskey was pushed his way. He tossed it back as Grim joined him.

By his stiff posture, I didn't think this would be solved overnight.

I tore my gaze away, tempted to run outside to join Talon.

Raven must have noticed where my thoughts led. "Gotta stay here. You leave now, and you make it worse."

I sagged against the cushion with his reply.

"Talon did what he needed to do," Raven explained. "He tore off the band-aid quickly so it wouldn't be as painful later."

"I don't get it."

"You will, honey. I promise. It's gonna make sense once we're back at The Roost."

I hoped he was right. It was going to be a long night without Talon. His warmth chased away nightmares and helped me sleep. Once we got to the Devil's Murder clubhouse, I hoped this would get sorted out because I wanted to be with Talon.

Crow couldn't stop us from being together. Right?

TALON

FUCK. FUCK. FUCK. I lit up a smoke outside The Crossroads, delaying the inevitable. I had to leave.

I wouldn't disobey an order from my pres.

But *fuck*, it hurt to ride off without Gail.

"It won't be easy."

I turned my head, nearly dropping my cigarette, when I saw Carrion leaving the shadows. "Goddamn. You sneaky fucker."

"Everyone acts like they don't know I use the shadows."

"Yeah, well, I guess it never loses the element of surprise."

Carrion actually laughed. "Maybe you're right."

I took a long pull on my smoke. "So? What won't be easy?"

"You'll know when the time is right."

"Do you always have to be so fucking cryptic?" I asked, flicking ash to the ground.

"You have no idea, brother." He cleared his throat. "It won't be easy, but you can do it."

More crazy shit to decipher?

"I'll remember that."

He tilted his head to the side as he listened for something I couldn't hear.

"Are you riding with me?"

He stared out into the desert. "No. I've got somewhere else to be. Right now."

I opened my mouth to reply when I saw him step into the shadows and disappear. Giant ebony wings flapped above my head, and I knew it was Carrion. A soft kraa followed.

Well, fuck. I guess it was time to head out. If I didn't soon, Crow would kick my ass. I turned to The Crossroads, already missing Gail. She became everything to me, and I had to find a way for Crow to see that.

I knew he'd witness our kiss. That was the plan. The sooner he understood my feelings about his sister, the easier this shit would be to hammer out. I wasn't walking away from her.

He needed to learn that.

I flicked the butt of my smoke to the ground, watching as the cinders sprayed across the asphalt.

It felt like a part of me stayed behind when I rode out of the gate and merged onto Hwy 95. It would take three and a half hours to reach home and The Roost. I knew I would spend all of them thinking of Gail.

About halfway through the trip, I realized I needed gas. We usually filled up in Tonopah before we left when the club stopped by The Crossroads, but I didn't think about it. Too distracted.

I took the next exit and found a gas station, filling the tank on my Harley while I pulled out my phone and texted Gail. I didn't expect her to answer.

She sent a heart emoji and lips. *Cute.*

The nozzle clicked, and I pulled it from my tank, placing it back in the cradle. I spun the cap, threw a leg over my ride, and returned to the highway. Headlights appeared behind me, but I didn't think anything of it. Pulling back on the throttle, I increased my speed.

The vehicle approached, matching me, and getting far too close to a motorcycle to be a safe distance.

I ignored the glare in my mirrors and sped up again. The truck did the same.

Well, fuck.

The engine revved behind me. . .and then bumped my back tire. I managed not to swerve hard, but that shit wasn't an accident. Someone wanted to force me off the road.

This time, I was ready when the truck revved again. I swerved hard left, picking up speed as I zipped down the highway and ditched the truck in my dust.

Asshole. What the fuck was that about?

It never occurred to me that whoever drove that truck didn't work alone.

I realized too late that another vehicle was headed my way, facing me in my own fucking lane. I veered left. He followed. I veered right. He copied my movement.

Motherfucker!

The previous truck caught up just as the one in front blinded me with his lights. I only had one choice. One chance to get out of this alive.

If I moved too slowly, I would end up the squished condiment in a pickup truck sandwich.

I thought of Gail and how I couldn't save her in this scenario.

I'm so glad you're not with me, baby.

The trucks kept racing toward one another, and a head-on collision. I hoped my leathers would protect my skin. Thank fuck I wore a helmet.

And that was when I released the handlebars and leaped from my Harley, not daring to look back at her destruction. I ragdolled, airborne, until I slammed into the unforgiving asphalt. The impact was fucking brutal. I lost count of how often I rolled, bouncing multiple times as I felt a few bones crack in the process.

Fuck. A groan escaped as I tried to move, to breathe, and agony fired along my chest. Looking down, I found a small stick embedded in my chest. It wobbled as it stuck straight up in the air.

Did I puncture a lung?

Caw...caw.

The crow. He sensed danger, agitated by the presence of our enemy.

Intense hatred vibrated nearby. I could feel it.

The crow's round body dropped from the sky, landing at my feet. Ruffling his feathers, he began to croak and kraa for his brethren, but there was nothing I could do. I didn't have the same ability that Hawk and Carrion did.

It won't be easy.

Carrion's words echoed in my head.

It won't be easy, but you can do it.

What the fuck did he mean?

It didn't matter. I wouldn't be awake long enough to figure it out.

"Gail," I coughed, turning my head as I choked, tasting the coppery tang of blood.

Raven and Carrion would know Gail was my mate. They would convince Crow. She would be safe. Protected. That was all that mattered.

My eyes shut, and I lost the battle to remain awake, falling into the arms of an endless dark abyss.

Chapter 10

GAIL

IT WASN'T LONG BEFORE Crow turned my way, watching as I folded my arms across my chest and scowled. I didn't hear his sigh, but I could tell he did.

He picked up two beers and walked in my direction, ticking his chin toward a hallway that led to the right. Since I wanted answers, I followed him. We entered a private room that looked reserved for important meetings. Framed leather vests hung on the walls. A giant grim reaper, molded from steel, suspended on the farthest wall and loomed over the wooden table in the center. In the middle of the table, a skull with a beard and crown had been etched into the surface.

"This is the chapel," Crow informed me, closing the door as he entered. "It's where the club holds meetings. We call them church."

"You have a chapel at The Roost, don't you?"

"Yeah. It's similar to this one."

He handed me a beer and sat at the table, ticking his chin at the chair across from him.

I sat, rolling the bottle between my palms. "Why did you send Talon away?"

Crow popped the top off his beer and took a long swallow. "I needed to make a point."

"What point would that be?"

Crow leaned back in his chair. "Rules aren't negotiable, and neither are a president's orders."

"And you ordered him to stay away from me?" I didn't understand biker politics.

"No," he replied, gripping the beer as his knuckles turned white. "I told him to keep his cock in his pants, and if he touched my sister, I'd rip off his fucking dick."

"Are you serious right now?"

"You think I'm not?"

I picked up the beer and threw it at him.

Crow ducked, dodging the bottle as it hit the wall and shattered behind him. "The fuck was that for?"

"For messing with my love life," I seethed, "for pushing away the first guy that made me feel like I was the most beautiful woman in the world. I think he might love me."

Crow's eyes widened, then narrowed. "You're not hooking up with a biker."

"Excuse me?"

"No. Fucking. Bikers."

I stood and glared at Crow. "How dare you think you have the right to dictate a single thing in my life."

"Abigail," he sighed.

"No. Don't. I don't even *know* you, Austin."

"This—"

I didn't let him finish. "Why the hell do you think you can order me around? I'll just walk away. I'll fucking run and—"

He shoved away from the table and closed the distance between us, throwing his arms around me. "Don't say that. Please."

The broken way the last word left his lips dissolved my anger.

"Austin."

"I'm not good at this. Okay? I'm not used to feeling so overprotective. First, Bella. Now, you."

"Bella?"

"The sexy as fuck brunette I fell in love with. My ol' lady. I've known her for six months, Gail. She's my *everything*."

"And you want to keep me from finding the same thing?"

He flinched. "Fuck."

"Yeah. *Fuck*." I rested my cheek over Austin's heart.

Neither of us moved for a full minute.

"How pissed are you?" He stepped back, staring at me with a vulnerability I never expected.

"I'm a five out of ten."

He grunted.

"It used to be ten, so we're making progress."

He almost smiled.

"You know I love you, right? The fucking second I found that birth certificate and learned I had a sister, I knew I had to be the big brother you never had."

Crow *cared*. My brother, Austin Derek Holmes, acted like a big, overprotective, ridiculous asshole because he wanted to protect me. Tears welled in my eyes.

I shook my head, but I couldn't stop them from overflowing. "Austin."

He pulled me back into his arms and awkwardly patted my back. "Fuck, Gail. I didn't mean to make you cry."

"This is one thing you don't have to be sorry for," I sniffled.

"It doesn't matter to me if we have different mothers," he added. "There's no half to me. We're blood. That's it."

I loved that he felt that way. I did, too.

"I agree."

We separated, and I brushed the wet streaks from my face. "So now comes the hard part."

"Oh?"

"You have to answer my questions."

"Shit," he laughed, "I bet you have a lot of them."

"I do." I pointed to the table. "Sit."

We both returned to our seats. Crow picked up his beer and finished it, pushing the empty bottle aside. "Alright. Go."

"What's your favorite color?"

He blinked. A wide grin appeared. "Red. Like Bella's lips."

I wrinkled my nose. "Ewww."

That earned a chuckle. "What's yours?"

"A blue summer sky." Just like Talon's eyes.

"Favorite food?"

"Pizza. Anything Italian."

He smirked. "Me too."

This felt good. I wanted to get to know my brother. "Favorite movie?"

"Star Wars."

"Original trilogy," I guessed.

The corners of his eyes crinkled. "Yep."

I knew it. "It's a tie with Lord of the Rings."

"Oh, damn. You're right."

I sat back, tracing the wooden pattern on the table. "How did Rook die?"

A strangled sound left my brother's throat. I lifted my head, biting my lip, when I saw the sorrow in his eyes. "Murdered."

My body stiffened. "Who?"

"The Dirty Death MC. Their president, Undertaker."

"Why?"

"I don't know," he admitted, forming a fist before slamming it into the table. "It doesn't matter. I'll find him, and I'll end him, Gail. I swear our father will have justice."

I nodded, slumping back in my chair.

Crow stood. "I'm getting a few beers. Want anything?"

"Yeah. Something diet."

"You got it."

When he returned, he placed a couple of diet sodas and a bottle of water in front of me—six beers for him.

"So," he began. "How often did Uncle Derek visit you?"

"Most of my life. I don't remember a time when he wasn't around. I always saw him for my birthday and holidays. Even if he didn't stay long, he made sure that he showed up."

"That sounds about right."

"He made everything better, Austin." I wondered how much to reveal about my childhood. It wasn't terrible, but it had some rough years.

"Tell me. Whatever it is, I want to know."

"My stepdad, Ross. He was an asshole."

Crow narrowed his eyes. "What did he do to you?"

"Physically? Nothing."

Crow's lip curled into a snarl. "What. Did. He. Do."

"He insulted me. Made fun of me. Ross wasn't happy unless he was picking on me or adding extra chores for me to do. I used to think he would make messes just so that he could tell me to clean them up."

"Motherfucker. Is he still around?"

"I think a man that mean will survive a long time."

"Where is he?"

"It doesn't matter. I don't have anything to do with him or my mother. She let him get away with all that mental abuse."

He didn't like that answer but didn't push it.

"My mother left when I was a kid. Just took off one day and decided I wasn't enough reason to stay."

Wow. "I'm sorry, Austin."

He shrugged. "I don't have a lot of memories with her. They're mostly about my pops, the club, and all the brothers who taught me shit I shouldn't know too early in life."

I had to giggle at that.

"What's going on with my house and my car?"

"I have a prospect watching the place. He texted me a couple of hours ago. No one has been there since you left."

It dawned on me that I was probably fired. I called off for a few days but never followed up. Things got crazy fast. And then Talon made me forget all my worries.

"What?"

"I'm not going to be able to pay my bills. I'll lose my house."

Shit.

"All taken care of."

My gaze snapped to his. "What do you mean?"

"I paid off the mortgage."

I stared at him, unable to process what he said. "You paid off my mortgage?"

"Yes."

"I had fifteen years left on that loan, Austin."

"I'm aware."

"I don't, wow. That's too much."

"No, it's not. I didn't get to be there for you. We didn't grow up together. Dad would have wanted to help."

"He did. Uncle Derek was my co-signer."

Crow shook his head as he smirked. "I bet."

"What about the body in my bedroom?" I cringed as I remembered the sinister look in those dark eyes.

"There's no trace of him."

"So. . ."

"It's taken care of. No one will ever know he was there, and they won't find him either."

Damn.

"Why did he come after me, Austin? I don't understand why my house was targeted."

"It wasn't the house. Nick Grime and his brother Luke work for Undertaker."

"Nick?" Like the guy I went on a date with? That Nick?

"Talon confirmed Nick was the guy in your house."

"Shit. What about his brother?"

"We haven't located Luke yet. I think he's hiding out while the heat dies down."

"He's going to be pissed about his brother."

"I believe so, yes. I'm counting on him to fuck up and come around, so I have a reason to end him too."

"You talk about killing like it's easy."

"Never easy but sometimes necessary to protect the people we love and the life we lead."

"Is that how it is? Being a biker?"

"There are days like that, yes."

He told the truth. I respected that, even if his answer bothered me.

"That's why you're the president," I realized. "You have strong shoulders for that burden."

Crow sat back, stunned. "That's what Rook said a month before he died. Word for word."

"Then I guess we're both right."

"Yeah."

"Austin?"

"No question is a stupid one."

Good to know.

"Why do the crows follow us?"

My brother finished off a beer and wiped across the back of his mouth. "Tell me what you mean."

"I hear them around me all the time. They caw and hop around on the roof of my house and at the pharmacy where I work. I see them land when I go to the grocery store or pump gas."

His brow lifted, but he didn't say anything.

"I feel soothed by their presence the same way Talon comforts me. But this started a long time ago. I used to notice the crows following Uncle Derek."

"You're observant. That's good."

"And it's not an answer."

"Gail. This will sound crazy."

"I think I can handle it."

He didn't argue.

"The crows are linked to the club and its members."

Linked? "How?"

"We're bonded. Soul-bonded."

I tilted my head, staring at him as I waited for Crow to tell me he was joking. He didn't.

"A bond? How does that work?"

"Try something for me. Close your eyes."

"Austin."

"Do it."

I closed my eyes, thinking of Talon.

"Tune out everything else around us. There's no one here but you and me."

"This is silly."

"Come on. Try."

The clubhouse disappeared, and I heard the sound of my breathing and Crow's voice, nothing else.

"Do you hear them?"

"No. Wait. Yes. I can see them."

"What?"

Through a slight haze, I viewed the night sky. Stars twinkled around me in every direction. Wings spread out at my sides as I glided on a current of wind. The moon lit the clouds above my position, and I found the others following my lead. Urgency filled my chest. I had to bring the murder.

Talon. Hurt. Help.

The words weren't my own.

My vision clouded, and I blinked, staring at Crow.

"What did you see, Gail?"

"The murder. It's flying toward Talon." I swallowed. Hard. "He's in danger."

Chapter 11

UNDERTAKER

"FIND HER!" I BELLOWED, snarling at my beta. "Now!"

The moment I awakened, my eyesight returned. I woke on a soft tuft of grass, groaning with the memory of seeding and claiming my mate. And the proof lay all around me.

The tattered remains of Sadie's dress. Her blood. My cum.

I would find her. That was a certainty. Wherever she ran, it would never be far enough. No hunter was greater than the vargulf.

I knew the fool who helped her to escape from me used his métier again. Carson Phillips had a secret. He could channel magic from the earth and summon it, bending it to his will. I chained him in the prison my pack built a century ago for those who tried to hunt us down, intrigued by the hum of energy always present around him. Carson remained in that jail cell for months until I brought Sadie to him, ordering him to sever their bond.

He used his ability to blind me, and Sadie ran.

But I caught up to her, claimed her with my mating bite, and bound her to me forever. Whatever hold Carson had over her, it had to be removed now.

Once they were located, I would let the vargulf have his kill. Carson would die for his treachery. He escaped that prison cell and I wanted to know how the fuck he managed it. Why wait for months as a prisoner to finally break free now?

Sadie. For her.

A dark chuckle left my lips.

How sacrificial and noble. Pathetic.

For now, I sent my pack to hunt. They needed the distraction. Our losses created tension, and the wolves needed an outlet for their frustration and anger.

I paced the length of my den. Over three hundred years ago, my ancestor and alpha to the pack settled this stretch of land on the border of Nevada and California—a home for the vargulf and his pack.

And we defended it viciously.

It was part of the reason I hated the Devil's Murder MC. Those crows were always in the way. I killed Rook, their president, hoping to teach them a lesson. Back. Off.

It didn't work.

So. . .now I would take them all down—one at a time.

A war that would end in bloodshed and one victor. *Me.*

I knew every safe location they had, every home the members lived in, and everywhere they met on a regular basis. The Roost, their clubhouse. I couldn't get the stench of those fucking crows out of my nose, which pissed me off and agitated the vargulf.

Maybe I would let him eat them all and crunch their bones into dust.

"Alpha."

I turned with a snarl, staring at a member of my pack. A young wolf who proved his loyalty daily. "What is it?"

He kneeled before me, keeping his head lowered and his neck exposed. "You have a visitor. Luke Grime."

"Send him in."

"Yes, Alpha."

I reached for a bottle of whiskey and twisted off the cap, chugging several swallows as the burn slid down my throat.

"Undertaker."

"Why are you here?" I growled.

Luke and his brother Nick were pests. I didn't care that one of the Devil's Murder members had murdered Nick. He was unworthy.

"I brought you a gift."

Intrigued, I set the whiskey aside. "What gift?"

I only had two interests: a hole to fuck or an enemy to eviscerate. The vargulf was in a mood.

"I think it's best to show you."

The vargulf didn't like surprises. His anger rumbled my chest.

"I promise this is a gift you'll enjoy."

"If you're wrong, I will feast on your entrails."

TALON

EVERYTHING HURT. EVERY part of my body pulsed with waves of agony that relentlessly pounded into my skull, stealing my breath whenever I attempted to move.

The pain was what awakened me. It assaulted my senses and lashed at each nerve. Just breathing stole me from consciousness, and I had no idea how many hours or days I struggled and fought to clear the fog in my head.

My eyes cracked open, and I could see the white crescent of the moon's shape through the window above my head. Stars twinkled in the dark sky but didn't help me remember where I was or how I arrived there.

Steel bars lined the room across from where I stood, anchored to the wall. Someone shackled my wrists and ankles using long ropes of thick chains. To my left, a dirty cot beckoned, promising comfort, but I didn't have the energy or the ability to reach it. The chains were too taut.

That was probably a good thing because the chains had to be the only thing keeping me upright. I glanced down the length of my torso, cataloging my injuries. Dirt and dried blood crusted over my skin in multiple spots. My bare chest was mottled with bruises. No shirt and no cut.

Fuck.

I scanned the cell and found my cut thrown on a wooden chair with a busted leg and spattered with bloodstains. It tilted at an odd angle, but at least my colors weren't on the fucking dirty floor.

I tried to suck in a breath and wheezed. A tiny rattle in my chest followed. And then. . .*pain.*

The edges of my vision blurred. When my head fell forward, I knew I would pass out again.

The endless cycle continued. I would wake, attempt to breathe or move, and lose the fight, tumbling into blissful rest where the pain couldn't reach me. In those moments, Gail appeared.

Every single fucking time, I would end up in that barn with her again. Her warmth would surround and comfort me. I would feel her soft skin beneath my fingertips and the plunge of my cock into her welcoming, tight pussy.

Torture. Every time it happened, I woke in the cold, empty cell. At some point, an IV had been stuck into my right arm. The hydration, what little trickled into my veins, kept me alive. I knew I had lost time. It had to be days—maybe weeks.

My stomach grumbled as my head lolled, hanging as I lacked the strength to lift it. Would I rot in here and never see Gail again?

Gail. Beautiful. I need you.

Cold water splashed my face, and I woke with a jolt, staring into unfamiliar eyes.

"There you are, you stinky fucker. Awake now, huh?"

I stared at the asshole with sandy brown hair and cold, dark eyes. "Who are you?" I asked, slurring my words.

"Ah, not yet."

"What do you want? Why am I here?" I tugged at the chains but didn't have the strength to do more than rattle them against the stone wall.

The stranger smiled. "Don't worry. That will become clear soon enough."

He lifted his hand, bringing the object he carried closer to my face. I stared at the propane torch and understood what he meant. No amount of preparation would help ease the pain that followed.

When the flame touched my skin, I screamed. I couldn't prevent it. My flesh sizzled and burned as bile rose in my throat. I passed out when he moved to a new area of exposed skin.

A hand slapped my face. "Talon. Wake up!"

My eyes fluttered, and I blinked. With my return to consciousness, the pain intensified. Not even when I blacked out did it fully recede. I barely noticed the IV was out of my arm.

"We have an audience today."

I didn't know what this asshole meant until my gaze found the steel bars and the monster who stood behind them.

Undertaker.

I should have guessed he would be involved. My lip lifted in a snarl. I would kill him for this. Ad the fucker in front of me? He'd die first.

Undertaker grinned as we stared one another down. "Had enough yet, Talon?"

"Fuck you."

"Ah, but I prefer pussy. Maybe Crow's sister next time."

I stilled. My body froze as the terrifying thought they managed to capture her nearly broke me. He had to be lying. Crow would never allow anything to happen to Gail.

Wait. That was what this was about? The fucking Grime brothers? Memories flooded my brain. Gail's house. The two months I watched over her. Nick showing up and putting him down. Getting Gail to the safe house.

I turned to the asshole in front of me. "Luke."

"I knew you would figure it out."

Undertaker opened the cell and walked in. "Tell me where it is."

I stared at him in confusion. "What are you talking about?"

He moved closer. "You have to know."

I didn't have a clue what the fuck he meant.

"You don't. Interesting." Undertaker stood there, unmoving, like he was deciding something in silence. "Rook has something of mine. I want it back."

"I can't give you what you want. He's fucking dead, you piece of shit," I yelled, letting the rage I felt about Rook's murder take over.

"You'll tell Crow I want it back, or I'm coming for Abigail, Bella, Callie, and Bree. I'll rotate fucking each of them in every hole until I get what I want."

A roar launched from my throat as I pulled on the chains, seething with fury.

How fucking dare this arrogant motherfucker threaten the Devil's Murder! "You won't get close enough to any of them to try."

A dark chuckle filled the stagnant air of the jail cell. "I will get what I want, little crow. One way or another."

"Fuck. You," I spat.

Undertaker turned to Luke. "Release him."

Luke's eyes widened before he shook his head. "No! I want justice for Nick! That's not—"

Luke's words cut off when Undertaker lifted his hands and twisted his neck, snapping it so fast it took a second for me to realize what he did.

Undertaker's shrewd gaze met mine. "Tell Crow."

How the fuck was I supposed to do that, chained to a fucking wall?

He stepped forward and yanked on the chains, busting them into pieces that scattered all over the dirt floor. I blinked as he reached inside his cut and pulled out a key, unlocking my wrists before slapping it into my hand.

"You have one week."

Nikki Landis

I didn't watch him leave, focusing on staying upright and conscious before I slowly lowered, propping myself against the wall as I unlocked the cuffs around my ankles.

Fuck. My vision blurred. I was too weak.

I'd never get out of here on my own.

I needed the crows.

Chapter 12

GAIL

CROW RUSHED TO HIS feet, striding toward the door and flinging it open. "Raven!"

The V.P. ran toward us, skidding to a halt before Crow. "What is it, pres?"

"Talon," he choked, shaking his head. "Gail saw the crows on their way to him. He called the murder."

"Shit."

Yeah, shit. But what did that mean?

Raven blinked. "Wait. She *saw* the crows?"

Crow nodded. "And she felt their panic."

Raven's gaze swung to me, widening as he cracked a smile. "Damn."

"You guys are weirding me out," I admitted.

Crow ticked his head toward the chapel. "Get in here."

Raven entered, and Crow shut the door. He started to pace, frowning as their gaze met again.

"Okay. Someone talk. Explain this to me."

Raven finally turned in my direction. "What you saw, that's not something anyone outside the Devil's Murder club members has ever seen. Do you understand what I'm saying?"

No. Not at all.

Crow glanced my way. "He means that crows only show themselves and what they can see to the one they bond with, which is always a club member. Most of us are born with the ability. A few haven't, but that's a conversation for another time."

Okay. I let that sink in. "So I saw the murder flying to Talon, and that's rare?"

"Not rare," Crow countered, "but impossible."

"Not really," Raven disagreed. "She's a Holmes. We've never had a woman bond to a crow, but that's because the crows already bonded to the club member first."

"And that's not any different now," Crow added.

"But she's your sister. She's Rook's blood. That must have changed the bond or altered it."

"I still don't get it," I sighed.

Raven turned to Crow. "She can do this because she's your blood, Rook's daughter, and she already bonded to a mate."

Crow stopped walking. He turned to Raven with narrowed eyes. "Raven."

"You're gonna have to accept it, Austin."

Damn. He used my brother's real name.

"She bonded to Talon and his crow."

My brother picked up a chair and flung it across the room. It smacked into the wall with a loud thud. Frustration and anger warred for dominance in his eyes. "I said no."

114

Raven shook his head and smirked. "It's already done."

Crow sighed. "Is that true?"

"If you're asking if I was intimate with Talon," I began.

"Fuck. I don't want to hear this," Crow muttered.

"What's so bad about me bonding with Talon? He's a good man. You know that, or you wouldn't have sent him to watch over me. He's trustworthy and sweet. I," I faltered, ignoring the sting of tears in my eyes. "I love him."

Crow growled. "You don't know him well enough to love him. He's a pain in the fucking ass."

"Only because he fell in love with Gail," Raven pointed out.

Crow sank onto the nearest chair. "Shit."

"You're not gonna stop this, Crow. They're mated."

"We are?" I asked, needing confirmation.

Raven nodded. "Yeah. That's the only reason his crow showed you the murder and what they intended. He considers you his mate, too."

Um, okay. Weird.

"So, let me get this straight. The Devil's Murder MC members are all bonded to crows. The crows connect to each one and share, what, abilities?"

"Basically, yes. Each crow also has one mate. When they find their one, that's it. They bond. . .for life."

Woah. "So Talon and his crow think I'm their mate because of fate or something?"

Raven shook his head. "It's more than fate. Close your eyes. Think of Talon. Tell me what happens."

Always with the eyes closing thing. I listened, focusing on Talon. The first thing I felt was warmth. Heat flooded my body and concentrated in my core, pulsing around my clit.

Damn. Talon's need and arousal were intoxicating.

And then affection bloomed in my chest. Awe.

Love.

Oh, Talon.

That faded too until all that remained. . .was pain.

I blinked, gasping as I looked at Raven, then Crow. "He's in pain. Talon's hurt." The panic in my voice unsettled both men.

"Fuck," Raven cursed.

"We need to find him. Now, Raven."

"They have him," Raven whispered. "Goddammit."

"Who has him?" I asked, looking between them. "Tell me."

"The Dirty Death MC. Undertaker."

"No." I shook my head, refusing to believe it. But it had to be true. Talon's pain leaked through our bond again, sinking through my chest and forming an ache around my heart. "He's injured. It's bad."

"We're leaving," Crow announced. He stood and moved toward me, sliding an arm around my shoulders. "We'll find him. I promise."

Within fifteen minutes, we were on the road, heading toward The Roost. Crow decided to drop me off first before he left to search for Talon. Raven agreed.

I wanted to look for Talon now. Neither man budged.

Fatigue set in during the journey, and I had to fight to stay awake and keep my hold around my brother's waist. Crow tapped my leg more than once to wake me up. He even lightly pinched me, and I felt his stomach shake with laughter.

Those were the longest hours of my life, riding until my ass went numb, worrying about Talon, and running through all the craziness my life had become since the day someone broke into my house.

It was nearly dawn when we rode through the gates and arrived at the Devil's Murder compound. I could barely stay awake when Crow parked his bike. At least it was close to a door. I stumbled as I stood and lifted off the helmet, handing it to my brother.

He hung it from the handlebars, giving me a funny look.

"You're not gonna make it, little sister."

"That's because my ass is draggin', big brother."

He laughed and then scooped me up, entering through the door as Raven held it open.

Only a few members were awake at this hour. A bartender who wore a prospect patch. Two older guys with graying beards sat at the bar, playing a card game as they slapped them down and one took a shot of dark liquor. And an older man with an oxygen tank next to his side held his gnarled hands around a porcelain cup. A tube connected to the tank, but he wasn't wearing a nasal cannula. He sipped on black coffee and greeted us with a wave.

"What ya got there, Crow? Looks like a little Rook."

Crow grinned. "The only woman I would ever carry around besides my Bella."

"Ah, this must be your sister."

"I'm Gail." I yawned. "Hi."

He shooed us away. "I'm Lucky Lou. We'll be talkin' later. Go get some rest."

Crow ticked his chin at Lou and took the stairs, walking up to a third floor. "When I learned about you, I converted this part of the clubhouse into an apartment. It's a home away from home, so you always have a place to stay when you visit me."

"You did?"

"Yeah." He cleared his throat. "I guess you'll stay with Talon instead."

I frowned, looking around at the décor. . .in shades of gray, white, and black. Modern but still feminine with splashes of color and floral accents. How did he know?

"I love it. Talon can stay here with me."

My brother gave me a squeeze and beamed a grin, placing me on the couch. "There's a bedroom with a walk-in closet, kitchen, living room, and a bathroom. All yours."

I reached over and kissed his cheek. "You're the best, Austin."

He looked happy. "Get some rest."

"I'll try."

"Do or do not. There is no try."

I shook a finger at him. "Don't start quoting Star Wars. You're already the perfect big brother."

He blinked and lifted his hand over his heart. "Love you, Gail Holmes."

"Right back at ya, Austin Holmes."

He reached into a pocket and plucked out a silver key, placing it on my palm. "Here's the key. I had two made. The only person who can come in without permission is me, and that's only if it's an emergency."

"Thanks." That was thoughtful and sweet.

He dipped his chin. "Goodnight, nightingale."

"A new nickname?"

"I figured you needed one. It fits."

"I like it."

"Good."

Neither of us could hide our wide, cheesy grins.

He stepped to the door, holding it open, when a gorgeous young woman with dark hair that became redder as it reached the curled ends and big green eyes ducked under his arm.

"Is this your sister? Finally?"

She didn't wait for an answer, rushing toward me. She had me on my feet, squeezing the life out of me in seconds. "Abigail!"

"Gail," I murmured at the same time as Crow corrected her.

She winked at my brother and turned a huge smile my way.

"I'm his ol' lady, Bella. Isn't that the weirdest thing to call the love of your life?"

I giggled. "Yeah."

"Wow. You're so beautiful, Gail. Crow has been unbearable for weeks waiting to bring you home. I'm so happy you're at The Roost."

"I think you're gorgeous. And thanks."

She squeezed again and backed away. "I'll let you sleep, but we're having tea tomorrow."

Tea. My gaze flicked over her black jeans with the rips and tears. Black tank top. Biker boots. She had so much ink she had full sleeves in vibrant colors on both arms. The girl was stunning. My brother was in love with her. I could see it.

"Sounds wonderful," I replied, hiding a yawn."

"Come on, Bella-mine. She needs rest."

I waved as they closed the door and sank against the soft, plush cushion of my new couch. The last thing I did was smile when I realized it was the same brand as the designer sofa in my house. . .and it wasn't slashed or ruined.

BELLA LET ME SLEEP until about three in the afternoon before she knocked and then barged in, flipping on lights and opening the curtains, exposing the window. Bright sunshine flashed me like high-beam headlights.

I squinted and tossed a pillow at her as she laughed. "Now, Gail. How am I supposed to make you my best friend if you won't get out of bed? Come on!"

Her enthusiasm and sweet words eliminated any worries I had about Bella. She monopolized the remainder of the afternoon, practically dragging me downstairs after my shower to sit at a secluded table with a chalkboard sign hanging above it. She'd used colored pieces of chalk to write on the clean, washed surface, and I giggled when I read what she had put.

Reserved for tea.

Bella & Gail.

Cock-free zone.

A bouquet of roses in a clear glass vase between us on the table matched the one she had drawn on the chalkboard. There was one more image, and I snorted as I sat, shaking my head at the circle with a line across it placed over a dick and balls illustration. Oddly enough, it was cute.

"If I don't specify, the fuckers around here will steal our shit. I've become stabby."

This. I needed this so fucking bad.

Laughter spilled from my lips, and I clutched my sides, highly amused by her wit, charm, and sweet nature—one hell of a combination. My brother had to be madly in love with Bella. There wasn't any other option.

"I'm sure you're right."

She winked. "I've got a special menu all planned. Be right back."

When Bella returned, she sat a hot bubbling quiche with melted cheese, mushrooms, and broccoli on the table. I inhaled the decadent aroma as my stomach rumbled.

She added a warm pan of cinnamon rolls with cream cheese icing drizzled over the top, a bowl of freshly cut fruit, and decorative China with polished silverware. One more trip added a red cast iron teapot with little matching cups and a plastic honey bear.

"I feel adequately spoiled," I announced as we filled our plates. "Oh my God, Bella. This is amazing," I gushed after taking the first bite of quiche.

"It was my Gram's recipe. Been in the family a long time."

"Don't ever lose it."

She smiled. "I won't. My sister, Bree, loves this quiche too."

"I can see why."

We ate silently, mainly because we both kept making yummy noises and enjoyed the food too much for conversation. Once finished and our plates pushed aside, Bella refilled our teacups.

I added a little honey to mine and stirred before taking a sip. "So, how did you meet Crow?"

"At the bar where I worked. He asked me to marry him as soon as he saw me." She laughed and shook her head. "He was so cocky and self-assured, so focused on me, and goddamn is he hot." She waved her hand at her face a few times. "That man is sin and sex and all bad boy. I love it."

"Um, that's great, and *ewww*," I added.

She snorted. "Yeah, I guess you didn't need to know that part."

"I get it," I replied. "I really do. That's how I feel about Talon."

"Girl, he must have been waiting for you. A wild man like him needs a good woman. I bet he fucking worships you."

"He calls me beautiful. Not just as a compliment but like it's my name and all he can think about when he stares at me. It's addicting to have someone so enamored with you."

"It is," she agreed. Her throat cleared, and she sipped her tea.

"What?"

"I wanted to say something, but I'm not sure if it's overstepping."

"Well, you have to go with it now," I laughed, "Don't leave me hanging like an unreached orgasm."

Bella laughed and nearly choked on her tea. "God. I hoped we would hit it off. I was so worried I'd be too much. I'm kind of a crazy, loud bitch."

"I think we're going to be best friends, just like you said." She looked relieved.

"Crow will be so happy."

"He will as long as he leaves me and Talon alone."

She gave me a knowing look. "So he's already started the big brother, overbearing, macho shit?"

"You have no idea."

"That's fine. I'll add to your cause. No pussy for him until he gets his head out of his ass. I'll use toys instead and make him watch."

I had tea in my mouth and sputtered, picking up a napkin to dab at my wet chin as I giggled. "Jesus, Bella."

"I know. I'm a rare breed."

"Austin has his hands full with you."

"Oh, honey, every hour of the day he can."

I gagged, which prompted her to grin.

"I'm okay," I added as comfortable silence stretched between us.

"This is a lot to take in. The club. My brother. Talon. Finding my house broken into and people after me." I sighed. "But I can handle this."

"And the shit about your dad? Never knowing about your brother?"

"It's life, Bella. Things happen out of our control."

"True."

"And I've found people who love and accept me, welcoming me into a family. It's wonderful."

"That's all I wanted to know. If you need a friend, I'm here. I mean that."

I didn't doubt her sincerity. Reaching for her hand, I gave her fingers a squeeze. "I know. Thanks, Bella."

"Anytime, love."

A WEEK LATER, WE still hadn't found Talon.

During that time, I spend most of my afternoons with Bella, getting to know the woman who would become my sister-in-law. In the mornings, I often saw Lucky Lou.

Crow joined me occasionally, but his focus remained on Talon, and I knew it bugged him that the crows hadn't led him to his enforcer. None of us quite understood the reason for the delay. I saw the crows. I had felt their urgency.

There was no way in hell I'd give up hope.

On the eighth day since Talon left The Crossroads, I walked into the kitchen, desperate for a cup of hot tea, and spotted Lou. I waved, held up a finger to let him know I would be there soon, and used the Keurig to boil water. Once I had a bag steeping in the mug, I headed his way.

As he'd done every day for the last week, he placed a plate of baked goods and a covered breakfast tray for me on the table.

"You're spoiling me, you know."

"I gather you need a little more of that in your life."

"How could you know that?" I asked, genuinely curious.

"Eh, an old fart like me sees things."

I giggled. "You're ornery."

"The ladies have never complained."

I laughed hard at that and uncovered my tray. Three strips of bacon, two scrambled eggs with cheddar cheese, a sausage patty, and two pieces of wheat toast lightly buttered.

"This is perfect. It smells amazing. Thanks."

"Save room for the cinnamon rolls, cream cheese and strawberry Danish, and the blueberry muffins."

"Lou. I can't eat all that."

He snickered. "I know. That's why I'm sittin' here."

"I think you come here for the food."

"Shhh. Don't tell my secret."

I ate most of the items on the tray as we talked about the weather and Lou's plans for the upcoming week. When I picked up a cinnamon roll and picked at it, he placed his gnarled hand over my own.

"He's comin' back."

"Talon?" I asked to clarify.

"Of course. He's your man."

"I'm worried," I admitted.

"Don't be. He might be hurtin', but he'll come back to you. Trust me. Ain't a thing that could keep that man away from you."

Lou never saw us together. His comment didn't make sense.

"You doubt me."

"No, not really. I just don't understand how you believe that when you never saw us together."

"Well, Gail, honey, I don't need to see you together. I know Talon. That boy has been restless and wild. He hasn't slowed down since I met him."

I could see Talon like that. He must have been a handful as a child.

"Known him most of his life," Lou continued. "His dad was a mean one, but that ain't Talon. Just the opposite. When Raven took him under his wing, I knew he'd turn out fine."

"He did," I agreed.

"And that's how I know he's comin' back. He's got to be head over heels for you, honey. With the way your brother has been scowlin', I'm guessin' he also believes it."

I shook my head, thinking of Austin. "Crow is stubborn."

"Like your daddy."

"I wish I knew Rook." My fingers wrapped around my mug. "You think he loved me, Lou? Is that why he kept me a secret?"

"I can't say what his reasons were, Gail, but I do know that man must have loved you something fierce to protect you the way he did. I don't doubt for a second that you and your brother meant everything to him."

"Thank you, Lou. I needed to hear that."

"Let it sink in, honey. Being loved is good for the soul."

Chapter 13

TALON

I HAD TO GET to Gail. It was the only motivation that
helped me push through the pain and forced me to keep
walking no matter how many times I stumbled.

Above me, circling in an ominous inky cloud of feathers, the
crows followed. There wasn't much else they could do. The
constant caws and kraas were almost deafening, but I
couldn't fly, and they couldn't walk.

My crow, the one I bonded with years ago, landed on my
right shoulder. He chittered as I fell to my knees. Again.

This was impossible. I would never make it to The Roost. I
didn't even know where the fuck I was. After I managed to
escape from that underground prison on Undertaker's land, I
tried to find a road. A highway. Anything.

You'd think after most of the night, I would find someone, or
they would stumble upon me. Nope. Didn't happen.

Fatigue pressed in from all sides as I struggled to breathe.

I couldn't die here. I refused.

My crow croaked in agreement.

It took every ounce of strength in my body to rise to my feet, and when I did, he hopped from my shoulder and got in my way. His wings rapidly flapped as he snapped his beak.

Crazy fucking bird.

"Hey," I groaned.

He kept making noise, acting pissed, until the whole damn murder joined us on the ground.

"Okay. What's the problem?"

They moved forward as if they were about to start mobbing, and I tripped, trying to move away, falling on my ass. Talons began latching onto my clothes and digging into my skin. I didn't know what they wanted.

And then. . .they tried to lift me.

The *fuck*?

Carrion's words pushed to the forefront of my mind. I couldn't remember when we spoke. Last week? Last month?

It won't be easy, but you can do it.

Did he mean. . .*fly*. . .with the crows?

Get the fuck out. I couldn't do that. Right?

I suddenly understood what he had tried to convey. It wouldn't be easy because I was injured, and I had to trust the crows, being vulnerable, which wasn't something an enforcer enjoyed. Carrion couldn't have been more specific. It wouldn't have made sense, and I would have challenged it, dismissing the possibility.

But I didn't feel that way now. I needed help. The crows were offering, and I couldn't refuse. If I didn't take the chance, I would die before I ever returned to Gail. That was unacceptable.

I turned to my crow, and he bobbed his head. "Sorry, bud. Let's go."

Chittering broke out among the crows before they began grasping my clothes and I was fucking glad that I found my shirt and cut before I left that prison cell. Dozens of black birds arrived, so many that I was covered and lost within their protective huddle.

And then we began to lift. . .higher. . .higher. . .until I no longer had to bear the weight of my broken bones.

This shouldn't be possible. How could they carry such heavy weight? I didn't understand, but I didn't have to for it to work.

There were things about my bond with the crow that defied logic. This was another to add to the list. And really, I didn't fucking care. Not if they took me to The Roost and back to Gail.

I couldn't say how long we remained in the sky, flying under cover of night and avoiding people or the highway. Everything became a blur. I'd never felt so weightless. And the pressure on my lungs didn't feel as heavy now.

When my back rested on hard asphalt, I knew I was home. Loud caws and flapping wings brought my brothers running outside. I searched the shocked faces of everyone who filed outside but didn't see the one I longed for.

Gail. Come.

There was an agonized cry I recognized as her voice, and then she knelt at my side, weeping as her fingers caressed my face. Soft, smooth lips brushed mine.

"Talon. Can you hear me?"

I wanted to answer. I tried.

My hand lifted, resting over her heart, but that's all I could do. My body went limp, and my brain grew fuzzy. Black rolled in from the sides of my vision.

I left her, but I knew when Falcon found and healed me, I would see her by my side when I awakened.

I WOKE DISORIENTED, WONDERING how much time had passed since the crows brought me home.

"Talon," Gail whispered. "Can you hear me?"

"Yes," I croaked, slowly opening my eyes. I saw Gail's face first and reached for her, needing that connection as much as I needed the air in my lungs to breathe. "I'm okay," I assured her, sensing her worry. "I'm here, beautiful."

She sighed. "I missed you." Her fingers curled around my hand. "I'm so glad you're back."

"Not going anywhere again, baby. Crow will have to accept we're together. I'm not walking away from you."

"Good. He needed to hear that from your lips."

"For fuck's sake," Crow growled. "This is nauseating." He scowled. "And annoying."

Gail peeked at him over her shoulder. "You promised."

Something passed between them, and Crow's features softened. "I remember, little nightingale."

"Wow. That was fucking weird," Falcon blurted, looking between Crow and Gail with a fat grin on his face. "I'm glad Talon's alive so we can all share our feelings."

Crow pinched the bridge of his nose.

Gail giggled.

I laughed, coughed, and nearly choked.

My woman, my beautiful mate, brought a straw to my lips. "Drink."

Cool, refreshing water flooded my mouth, and I swallowed, chugging it down until the straw was empty.

"Better?"

"Oh, yeah," I answered, tugging her closer. "I can show you."

Pink dusted her cheeks as she flushed. "Talon."

A wicked grin spread across my face.

"Uh, Talon," Falcon called.

"What?"

"I suggest you take it easy until our pres leaves the room."

I turned my head, catching the murderous expression on his face. "Just a sec, pres." I reached for Gail and pulled her against me. "Hey, beautiful. Need to tell you something."

"Oh? What's that?"

"I love you."

As long as I lived, I would never, ever forget the look on her face. Surprise. Delight. Awe.

Before she could reply, I claimed her mouth, kissing her until she had to pull back to breathe.

Then I turned to the man I considered a blood brother. "Crow. I love your sister. She's my mate. My fucking heartbeat. You need to know I'll fucking kill to keep her."

"I guess I can't argue with that," he sighed.

Gail turned to him. "You're okay with it?"

"I don't have a choice. You love him too."

I grasped her chin, forcing her to look into my eyes. "Do you? It's not too fast?"

Nikki Landis

She smiled, and it was so fucking breathtaking it almost hurt to see.

"I've loved you since the night you bought all that food and two chicken sandwiches for me because you didn't know if I wanted tomato and lettuce or not."

I couldn't help but grin. "You love me."

"I don't think I'll ever be able to stop," she admitted.

"Fuck. How did I get so lucky?"

She glanced at her brother. "Leave, Austin."

He shook his head. Sighed. Then nodded. "Fine." The reply didn't sound grumpy at all. Good for him. "We recovered your Harley. It's in the shop," he informed me before he opened the door and closed it behind him.

"Falcon? Is he okay? Medically cleared?"

Oh, I liked where this was headed.

Falcon chuckled. "Yeah. Whatever he feels up to," he paused with a wink, "is fine. I'll be back later."

Neither of us looked as he exited, too lost in one another.

"So, are you really feeling up for anything?"

I inhaled a deep breath, relieved not to feel the same level of pain as I had before Falcon healed me. He did good. My body would take some time to finish the healing process, but it wouldn't be long. Falcon's healing energy soaked into my skin and mended the bones, punctured lung, and stab wound. I wouldn't be running a marathon anytime soon, but fucking my woman? Hell yeah, I had no problem feeling *up* to that task.

"So ready, baby. Why don't you uncover me and find out?"

She reached for the blanket and tugged it from my body. A gasp left her lips, followed by a sob.

Well, shit.

I looked down and noticed all the bruises fading in various shades of blue, green, and brown. The stitches. Puckered skin from the healing burns. And a fuck ton of dirt. In fact, I didn't smell great.

Fuck. That was a buzzkill.

"Beautiful, I'm fine. It looks a lot worse than it is. Why don't we take a shower? I could use the help."

She sniffled and nodded, walking with me to the bathroom. I started the water and tested the temperature, ticking my chin at her when it was ready.

"Naked, baby. Now."

I pulled off my clothes, holding back a groan as my body protested the movement.

"Step in. I want to brush my teeth first."

"Okay."

I watched her plump, sexy ass enter behind the glass doors and step under the spray. *Fucking delicious.*

When I finished brushing my teeth, I rinsed my mouth and joined her. The hot water worked wonders on my sore muscles. I finally felt alive again, like *me.*

I soaped up fast, getting clean because I had an agenda, and it involved my woman's tight pussy and her moans of pleasure. Gail seemed to be on the same page. She lowered to her knees, leaning forward to kiss the tip of my cock. It jumped, jutting out from my body, eager for more.

Her fingers wrapped around my length as I groaned. Fuck. Her touch was so soft and yet firm at the same time. *Perfect.*

My hips bucked when her thumb brushed over the head. I couldn't help reaching for her and gripping her hair. Her beautiful gray eyes looked wild, hungry. Our gaze stayed locked as she swirled her tongue over the crown before her hand wrapped the base. In a single, earth-shattering moment, her mouth took me in, deep. *So fucking deep.*

A guttural groan broke free from my lips. I didn't know which I preferred at that moment. Her tight, sweet cunt. Or the wet, warm cavern of her mouth. Both sucked me in eagerly. And fuck, neither was sweeter or sexier than the other.

I became lost in her when she hummed around me, working me harder, and flicking her tongue inside the slit at my crown. Jesus. Christ. I fell against the tile.

Fuck. Fuck. FUCK!

I knew I tugged at her hair, pumping my hips, but I couldn't let this stop. I didn't want it to end.

This felt so fucking good.

I finally pulled her off my dick, lifting her as she rose to help me. Gail's legs wrapped around my waist while the head of my cock nudged her entrance. "I don't think I can be gentle."

"I don't need gentle. Just *you*."

I rolled my hips and then pushed inside her, deeper, deeper, until I bottomed out. There was no way I couldn't move. She felt too warm and inviting. Too soft and tight and wet.

My hips receded for half a heartbeat and snapped forward. We were both lost after that. I gripped her ass, pulling her into me with every driving thrust. The world didn't exist anymore—only us.

Her fingers tangled in my hair as our mouths fused. Our kisses were wild, our tongues colliding, carnal, and messy. It was fucking everything we both needed. I knew the second she was going to come. Her breaths grew ragged, and her thighs locked around my waist. She moaned. . .and fucking shattered.

My release followed seconds later, and I growled, shuddering and holding her to me until I collapsed against her, completely sated. Fuck. Sex with her was unlike anything I ever experienced with another woman. No comparison.

"Love you, beautiful," I whispered against her mouth.

"I love you, Talon."

Chapter 14

GAIL

"Is Talon still sleeping?"

I joined my brother for breakfast, sliding across from him as I watched him dunk toast in egg yolk and then scoop egg on top before taking a bite. "Yes. He would never admit weakness, but he needs the rest."

"No crow would," he answered as he swallowed.

"True." I took a sip of tea and placed the mug on the table. "I've been thinking about what Carrion said."

"Which part?" Crow gulped coffee and emptied the mug. He pushed his empty plate aside. "Remind me."

"He said Rook left something for me."

"Oh, that." Crow shrugged. "If he did, I wouldn't know. It would be crazy to find something hidden around here. There's no goddamn privacy."

"I guess you're right."

"But, if you want to search The Roost. Go for it. No one will stop you. If they try, send them to me."

"That wouldn't end well."

"Exactly."

"I have this weird feeling in my gut."

"Weird, how?"

"Like we're supposed to walk into the basement."

Crow sat back. "I don't think that's a good idea. You don't want to see what we keep down there."

"I know it's probably old junk," I began.

"No, nightingale. It's where we use force to get information."

Oh. Yuck. "Is there blood?"

"Bloodstains, maybe."

I wrinkled my nose. "Then you're coming with me."

He sighed. "Alright. Let's go."

"Right now?"

"Right now."

Crow pushed up from the table, and I followed him, snaking our way through the other tables and exiting the dining area. He held out his elbow, and I looped my arm around his, smiling at the man who earned his big brother status more every single time we spoke.

"You're an amazing big brother, you know."

"Yeah?"

"Perfect, actually, even when you're a huge pain in the ass."

"Good to know," he laughed.

"I want to have Talon's babies, by the way. Just thought you should know," I blurted, watching him as I spoke.

He tripped over his feet, stopped, glared at me, and narrowed his eyes. "No babies. You're too fucking young."

I couldn't help the giggles that erupted. "Oh my God. Your expression is priceless."

"Are you saying that you don't want his babies?" The words sounded hopeful.

"Not for a long time, Austin."

"Thank fuck."

Crow unlocked a door and led us down the stairs, turning left. "There're only interrogation rooms to the right. No point going into those."

"Icky stuff?" I asked.

"All icky stuff."

I got my brother to say icky. Hilarious.

We stopped in a storage room as Crow pulled on a string, and a light bulb lit up the space.

"There's not much here except junk. Old shit of Rook's. Mementos. Leftover supplies from parties. I don't know how you would begin to sort through it all."

"Me either. I feel like I'll just know."

"That easy?"

"Well, yes." I let go of my brother's arm and walked around the room, stopping to stare at all the shelves and boxes. "It's not in here," I finally announced. "Anywhere else to look?"

"There's a bathroom down here, but nobody uses it. It has an old linen closet next to it."

"Show me."

Crow led the way, taking another path that I wouldn't have seen without his guidance. It was too dark, even with the bulb hanging in the middle of the storeroom.

He stopped as we rounded a corner, and a little nook appeared next to a tiny bathroom that only had a sink, mirror, and toilet inside. You could see every inch from the open doorway. Next to it, as he had already said, a linen closet stored supplies.

I felt drawn to the door and opened it, almost cringing when it squeaked on the hinges. I didn't know what I was supposed to find. It didn't make sense, but I felt Uncle Derek's presence. Rook was with us in spirit.

"Help me take everything out."

"Gail."

"Just do it, Austin."

He grumbled but started stacking rolls of toilet paper and paper towels, bars of soap, and other supplies.

I tapped my phone and touched the flashlight icon, turning it so the beam lit up the interior of the closet. There, in the back, my name was scrawled with a black marker. It stood out against the light brown wood, but it would never have been seen without adequate lighting, especially if someone had only stacked more things in front of it.

"Holy shit."

I slid my hand to the back of the shelf, feeling along the wood with my fingertips. I must have applied the right kind of pressure because I heard a little snap, and the wood broke free. A considerable chunk flopped onto the shelf. I picked it up, fascinated when I turned it over, and found folded paper notes taped to the back.

"Austin."

"I see it, Gail."

I slowly pulled the papers loose, realizing they were letters. Well, two of them were. The other was some kind of land deed. I handed one of the notes to my brother and opened the one in my hand. Handwriting that I recognized as belonging to Uncle Derek stared back.

Dear Austin,

Son, if you're reading this, it means I'm already dead.

"This one is yours."

"Same."

We switched.

Dear Abigail,

If you're reading this, I failed you.

Oh, shit.

I sucked in a breath as Crow reached out, clasping my hand.

We read our letters at the same time.

>*I bet you're wondering why I kept you a secret.*
>
>*That answer is simple.*
>
>*I knew he would come for you.*

He? Who?

>*Undertaker is evil. He won't stop until he eliminates everyone I love.*
>
>*That means you. Your brother. Your mother.*
>
>*I had to keep you safe.*
>
>*We decided no one could know about you.*

Wait. He wrote this letter a year ago. I could see the date.

My father hid me away as a child. This didn't make sense. The timeline was off.

"He says he met Undertaker as a young man."

"He did?"

"And he says you'll be confused, so I need to explain."

"Okay."

"Finish your letter, and we'll talk about it."

I know all of this will shock you.

You thought I was your uncle.

But, Abigail, I'm your dad.

I wanted to tell you so many times but couldn't risk it.

Undertaker swore vengeance. I knew one day he would try to kill any children I had.

Crow is strong. I've helped him become the man who can protect you. He's the right president for the club and your big brother.

Trust him. Please.

And try to forgive me for my sins.

I will always love you. You're my baby girl.

Keep singing, nightingale.

"Oh, shit," I blubbered. "Austin."

"I know," he answered, hugging me against his side. "He's right, you know. I won't let anything happen to you."

"What did he do to Undertaker?"

"Rook says it was an accident. He didn't see Undertaker's son until it was too late. A motorcycle crash that took his life. He's sorry he died."

"Oh, God."

"Undertaker wants us all dead because of a single mistake."

The unfairness of it, the horrible reality that a teenager died in an accident and his father couldn't handle it, swearing vengeance, nearly overwhelmed me.

"Austin?"

"Yeah?"

"Did you see how Rook signed my letter at the end?"

"No."

"Look." I lifted it in front of his face.

"Aw, fuck," he exhaled. "Damn."

"Right?" I didn't notice the tears streaking down my cheeks until my brother sniffled.

"It's so good you're here now. I didn't," he faltered, "I didn't know how much we needed one another."

"But we do."

"Yeah. I'm so fucking glad you're here, Gail."

Me too. No matter what reason brought me here, I knew I was supposed to join my brother. Our futures intertwined. "Our dad knew he had to bring us together."

"I wish it had been sooner, but we can't change that."

No, and that was okay. We were making up for it now.

I lifted the other piece of paper and flashed the light on it. "Oh, wow."

"Shit. What?"

"This is a deed. A legal document of ownership for a specific piece of land."

"Huh. I wonder if that's the reason Rook visited his lawyer the day he died. He sent our birth certificates and other legal documents, but not this. What property is it?"

"I think it belongs to the Dirty Death MC."

Crow reached for it, and I passed the deed into his hand. He stared at the document and laughed. "Holy shit. Undertaker doesn't own his fucking land. Rook paid the property taxes and stole it from him."

"That sounds dangerous."

"It is. No wonder we've been dealing with all this shit since Rook's death."

"I guess you need to have church now, huh?"

He slid an arm around my shoulder and hugged me against his side. "You're a quick learner, Gail. Yep. Let's go."

I had a bad feeling about this.

If Undertaker could hold a grudge this long about his son, he would never give up the control of his land to the Devil's Murder.

Chapter 15

TALON

CROW CALLED CHURCH INTO session, and before he could open up the floor or discuss what he had on his mind, I needed to tell him about Undertaker and the shit that went down in that underground prison.

"Undertaker gave me an ultimatum."

Crow's brows bunched together. "What kind of ultimatum?"

"He said we had something that belonged to him and had one week to give it back."

Crow laughed. "Fucking serious?"

"Yeah. Right after he twisted Luke Grime's neck and killed the fucker."

Raven whistled low next to me. "Fuck."

"It saved me the job of doing it," I snarled. "He fucking burned me with a fucking blow torch."

147

Crow slapped a palm on the table. "And kept you chained like a dog for a motherfucking week. This is on Undertaker. He'll get what's coming to him."

"For Rook, too," Raven growled.

Fists pounded the table in agreement.

Crow placed a piece of paper down and slid it toward the middle. "This is what he wants. The deed to his land."

"How the fuck did we get that?" I asked.

"Rook," Carrion answered from the corner of the room.

"He's right," Crow confirmed. "Rook paid the property taxes. Undertaker was behind thousands but not near what the land was worth. He lost millions in the transaction."

"Not to mention the ground where his clubhouse sits," Raven added.

"And the fucking underground prison."

"He's not getting it back," Crow announced. "I don't give a fuck how much he threatens us. We hold down this place and lock it tight. Keep watch over your families and women. He'll fight dirty."

"He always has," Hawk pointed out.

"So we'll be ready. He says he's giving us a week. We use that week to prepare."

Fists pounded the table a second time.

"This is war," Crow snarled. "We're defending The Roost with our lives. Every one of you needs to be ready. When Undertaker comes, he'll bring his pack."

"We can take them."

"The crows won't back down either."

"Justice for Rook."

I listened to my brothers but watched Crow. He seemed on edge. He wasn't saying everything.

There was something else on his mind.

"Church is dismissed."

The room cleared except for Crow, Raven, and me. I sat forward, bracing my elbows on the table. "What aren't you saying?"

"That easy to notice, huh?"

"To those of us who know you best, yeah," I answered.

"I'm worried about Gail."

That got my attention. "What do you mean?"

"She's manifesting some weird abilities. Things none of us have ever seen or heard about. She knew where to find the letters Rook had left us. The deed was with it. She went to the basement and found their hiding spot behind a hidden panel in a fucking linen closet."

"Wow."

"And when you were gone, Talon, she saw your crows. She connected to them. Gail knew you were hurt before any of us fucking knew you'd gone missing."

Holy shit.

"She's special," Raven agreed.

"And that means she'll intrigue Undertaker. He'll sense her abilities with that vargulf thing inside him. She's not safe here." He scrubbed a hand down his face. "She's not fucking safe anywhere."

"I'll protect her. I already swore that oath to you, pres. I love Gail. I'll defend her to the death."

"That's what worries me," he admitted.

"You think I'll fail?" Fuck. That sucked.

"No. But Undertaker isn't a normal wolf. He's a vargulf. Twice the size, cunning, strength, and rage. It'll take more than one of us to keep her safe from him."

"So what do we do?" I asked, rubbing at my chest and the sudden ache.

"We plan. And when the timing is right, we take her where he can't find her."

"And where the fuck is that?"

Anywhere she went, I'd follow. Nobody would get in my way, not her brother, or fucking Undertaker.

"I don't know yet, but I'll research everything I can until I do."

Carrion walked toward the table and pulled out a chair. "It won't work."

Crow sighed. "What part? I need more than that, Carrion. None of this vague, ominous shit where you don't give me any fucking answers."

"Fooling the vargulf. He can't be tricked."

"Okay," Crow replied, thinking it over. "What if we don't try to fool him? What if we keep her in plain sight?"

Carrion smiled. "There you go."

Plain sight. What the fuck did that mean?

Carrion turned to me. "You'll need to trust me again."

I nodded, knowing there wasn't much choice. "What do I need to do?"

"Stay out of it."

"You're asking me not to step in and protect my woman?"

"Her life depends on it."

Fuck! "Carrion. You can't ask that of me."

"I have to," he replied sadly. "If you don't listen to me, she won't make it."

He whipped his head toward Crow. "That goes for you too, pres. This is war. We're going to lose people. It can't be helped. But it's the specific *people* we'll lose that can be altered."

"Fuck."

"And that's a very tiny window open to keep Gail and Bella alive."

Crow stood on shaky legs. "Are you telling me I could lose my ol' lady and my sister?"

"Yes."

Crow shuddered.

"Do what I say when I say so. No hesitation. No argument. Just do it. The clock has already begun to count down."

In the entire time I had known Crow, I never saw him cry, even when he found out about Rook's murder. As I looked into his eyes, I saw fear, sorrow, and a fury that nearly stole the breath from my lungs. Tears brimmed in his eyes a few seconds before he blinked them back. He didn't appear weak because of it. It showed humanity, love, and a fierce commitment to protect the ones he cared about at any cost.

"We'll listen," I promised.

"Agreed," Raven added with a cough.

Crow hung his head, his breathing labored. When his chin lifted, I saw the resolution in his eyes. "I'll be ready."

Carrion never replied. He left, retreating to the shadows, but I caught the tear on his cheek as his gaze locked on mine.

I would never want the burden of his gift.

Knowing the future was its own torment.

Chapter 16

TALON

"I HAVE A CONFESSION to make," I murmured along Gail's neck, peppering kisses on the way to her jaw and pausing as I reached her mouth.

"That sounds incriminating."

"It is."

She laughed and swatted at my arm. "Tell me."

"You know those dates you went on?"

She blinked at me. "You didn't."

"I sure the fuck did."

"Talon."

"I ran every single one of those fuckers off because you're mine. I knew the first time I saw you."

"So you sent all my dates home? It wasn't me?"

"Nope. Not you at all."

She nodded. "That's good. I thought I was undatable."

"You were. I already claimed you." My lips brushed hers, and I backed away. "There's more."

"Okay."

"I hid under your bed one night, and I masturbated with you. It was fucking sexy to hear you getting off above me while I jerked off underneath you."

Her eyes grew wide. The prettiest pink blush darkened her cheeks. "Talon. I can't believe you did that."

"I'd like to do it again."

"Oh my God!" She hid her face in her hands. "When?"

Laughter rumbled in my chest. "I got such a naughty girl."

"Maybe you did."

I pulled her into my embrace, claiming her mouth again in slow, deep, intoxicating kisses. "You know shit is going to go down with the club, right?"

"I know."

"And there might be things we say, do, or ask that won't make sense to you."

"Okay. Are you asking if I'll behave?" She teased me, but this was serious.

"Baby, I need you to understand me."

Her expression betrayed a quick flash of fear. "I do. Whatever you need from me, or whatever Crow does, I'll do it."

Relieved, I nodded. "Good. That's all I need to know, Gail."

"Are you going to tell me what that means?"

"I can't yet. Will you trust me?"

"With my life," she responded. No hesitation.

"This is why you're so fucking perfect."

"Because I can behave like an adult?"

"No, because you're fucking sassy and strong, and you don't take shit from anyone, even me."

Her soft laughter warmed my heart.

I nuzzled her neck, so fucking thankful she was here. I didn't know what the fuck I would do if I lost her.

Whatever pact I had to make, or whatever the sacrifice, I would do it to keep Gail alive.

I pushed her back against the sheets, needing to be inside her after all the shit today. I had to feel her, to know she was safe and that nothing would take her from me. My head and my heart were at war, each trying to convince the other that she would be safe and that Undertaker couldn't get to her. But Carrion's warning lingered. I needed to get lost in my woman as I fucked her, and everything else faded away.

We were alive. We had each other, and we would fight to hold onto the love we found.

When she opened her legs and slid her hands into my hair, I groaned with need. When my cock entered her, and she welcomed me with that warm, wet heat, I knew I was home.

Whatever we faced in the future, we would do it together.

UNDERTAKER

A WEEK CAME AND went. No contact from the Devil's Murder. No news from Crow or any response to the ultimatum I freed Talon to deliver.

Did those fucking crows think I wasn't serious?

Did they believe I wouldn't seek retribution for Fang's life?

Rook fucking killed my son!

Rage colored my vision red, and my body vibrated with fury as hate slithered through my veins like acidic venom.

The vargulf threatened to rip me apart from the inside out. He seethed with the need for violence, and I had no desire to rein in the urge. I didn't even want to fuck. Only the uncontrollable lust for blood would cool the white-hot fury boiling within.

"Alpha."

"What?"

I turned to the three wolves, who bent low to the ground when my growl shook the walls. The trio whined under the pressure of my tone, baring their necks. I could use my claws and rip apart each of their throats within seconds, and all three sensed how I teetered on the balance of control. One wrong word, and they would all die.

"We found her," the youngest of the three announced.

"Your mate," one of the others confirmed.

"Where is Sadie? Tell me!"

"With the Devil's Murder MC. At their Roost."

A bellow of dark laughter burst from my lips.

Yessssss, the vargulf chuckled in my mind. *Perfect.*

I waved a hand, dismissing my pack members as they hurried to leave me and escape before I let the vargulf out to play.

Their fear was unfounded. I lost enough wolves to ensure I wouldn't needlessly dwindle those numbers further. They were safe. I needed the pack as equally as they needed me.

And with the war coming, I had to ensure they were ready to fight for our land and pack. To secure the future of our species, I needed my queen. She had to breed.

If fate favored me, then perhaps she had already conceived.

The thought drove the vargulf wild. He wanted to seed her again to ensure it took.

I forced his thoughts to retreat. My focus had to remain on the correct objective: vengeance, destruction, and then, my mate. She was in no danger among them. Sadie would be protected as if one of their own.

But they didn't know what I did.

They hadn't learned that the vargulf still held one ace. A way to ensure that the crows followed my demands and returned the deed to my land, signed it over, and left Nevada for good.

Of course, I would kill every last one of them before that happened, but it was a moot point.

Sadie would secure what I needed because she had no choice. The vargulf compelled her. After months in his possession, he finally broke through her mental walls and gained control. Not even her precious Carson could sever that connection.

Becoming my mate only cemented the bond further.

I strolled to the door and called for my beta. "Yes, Alpha?"

"When Bella arrives, bring her to me."

"Yes, Alpha."

I watched him leave, cracking a grin as I thought of every way that I would make Bella cooperate. It wouldn't take much. She was Crow's mate. Her bond with him had grown deep. A little pain would travel their link, and he would come for her.

Yes, Crow would bring the murder.

But he would never survive the bloodletting.

Epilogue

CROW

T HE HOUR HAD GROWN late by the time I returned to the room I shared with Bella. I'd spent far too many late nights away from her and guilt swept through me. I could tell she slept from the rumpled blankets on the bed, and I didn't want to wake her. The light was too dim to make out her features, but I didn't need to see her beauty to know my ol' lady was there.

I slowly stripped off my cut and draped it over a chair. My keys and wallet were placed on my dresser. Kicking off my boots, I sat on the edge of the mattress and reached for her, needing that tiny bit of connection to her to ground me.

Today, with Carrion's revelations, I had to hold her.

Something wet and sticky coated my fingers as I slid them over the large mounds, not feeling warmth or catching that unmistakable sweet scent of hers that always lingered in my room and on my clothes.

For a split second, terror overtook me. I couldn't move. I struggled to breathe.

My crow croaked outside, his throat rattling as he cried out.

And then I stood, rushed to the lamp, and flipped the switch, illuminating the room and my bed. Red. All I fucking saw was red. It splashed the walls. Streaked across the mattress. Stained everything in my vicinity.

Blood. *So much fucking blood.*

But it wasn't Bella. It wasn't human.

There, in the middle of my bed, was a fucking deer carcass. The throat had been slashed. It bled out on my sheets and comforter where Bella and I slept.

Someone would pay for this.

But where was my Bella? And why was her scent gone? Like she'd been erased? No hint of her perfume or body wash. No lingering sweetness or floral undertones.

I rushed to the bathroom. All her shit was gone.

Where. The. Fuck. Was. My. Woman.

I nearly panicked, rushing from my room and thundering down the stairs. My heart thudded against my ribcage as it beat so hard I thought it would crash through my chest. I entered the bar. . .and *total fucking chaos.*

Sadie, Callie's sister, stood beside a man I didn't know. They were covered in blood.

Deer blood? What the fuck was happening?

"Where's Bella?" I roared as the room grew quiet.

Everyone turned to stare, noticing the crimson stains on my hands and my jeans.

Sadie shook her head. "He took her."

"Who?" I growled.

"Undertaker."

My mouth opened, and agony unleashed. All the pain, fear, and rage I felt from Rook's death, combined with the knowledge that my enemy had taken my mate. My Bella.

She was gone.

A single word rumbled up my chest, bursting free from my lips.

"Kraaaaaa!"

There's much more to come with the Devil's Murder.

The next book in the series, **Crow's Revenge**, will be released in June 2024.

Undertaker's days are numbered.

Crow and Gail have a murderer to bring to justice.

Will they finally get vengeance for Rook?

Sadie, Carson, and Undertaker's fates are intertwined, and some revelations will change *everything*.

Watch for more in the Devil's Murder MC series.

You can read more about Grim and his club in the Royal Bastards MC Tonopah, NV Chapter, now available.

Find all Nikki's Royal Bastards MC and Devil's Murder MC books on Amazon and Kindle Unlimited.

Never miss out on a book! Follow Nikki on social media to receive updates.

#1 Crow

#2 Raven

#3 Hawk

#4 Talon

#5 Crow's Revenge

#6 Claw

#7 Cuckoo

#8 Carrion

#9 TBD

Love motorcycle romance?
Check out these books by Nikki Landis:

Royal Bastards MC Tonopah, NV
#1 The Biker's Gift

#2 Bloody Mine

#3 Ridin' for Hell

#4 Devil's Ride

#5 Hell's Fury

#6 Grave Mistake

#7 Papa Noel

#8 The Biker's Wish

#9 Eternally Mine

#10 Twisted Devil

#11 Violent Bones

#12 Haunting Chaos

#13 Santa Biker

#14 Viciously Mine

#15 Jigsaw's Blayde

#16 Spook's Possession

#17 Infinitely Mine

#18 Grim Justice

#19 TBD

Royal Bastards MC Las Vegas, NV

#1 Hell on Wheels

#2 Reckless Mayhem

#3 Jeepers Creepers

#4 Rattlin' Bones

#5 TBD

Royal Bastards MC Crossover

#1 Twisted Iron

#2 Savage Iron

#3 TBD

Ravage Riders MC

#1 Sins of the Father

#2 Sinners & Saints

#3 Sin's Betrayal

#4 Life of Sin

#5 Born Sinner

#6 TBD

Iron Renegades MC

#1 Roulette Run

#2 Jester's Ride

#3 TBD

Feral Rebels MC

#1 Claimed by the Bikers

#2 Stolen by the Bikers

#3 Snowed In with the Bikers

#4 TBD

Pres/Founder – Crow
VP/Founder – Raven
SGT at Arms – Hawk
Enforcer – Talon
Secretary – Carrion
Treasurer – Claw
Road Captain – Swift
Tail Gunner – Jay
Member/Tech – Eagle Eye
Member/Cleaner – Cuckoo
Member/Healer – Falcon
Prospect – Goose
Prospect – Robin

SNEAK PEEK

P ATRIOT LIT A CIGAR and puffed away, his eyes briefly closing as he inhaled. "Damn. Wraith's Cuban cigars are no joke. Pure fuckin' pleasure."

Wraith would be pissed when he saw Patriot smoking his expensive tobacco.

I snorted, grabbing a beer from the fridge. We found a private room with a pool table, minibar, and a few dartboards. Tables and chairs were scattered around the area, proving this clubhouse used all the rooms frequently. I popped the top and took a long pull from my bottle. Setting it aside, I picked up a dart, throwing it without aiming and hitting just slightly off-center.

"I'm too sober for this," I announced, giving him a smirk over my shoulder. Two more landed even farther from the bullseye.

"Fuck. I never see you miss." Patriot inhaled, closing his eyes briefly to savor the exotic taste and aroma. "This is almost heaven."

I shook my head. "Never thought I'd hear you say anything was closer to heaven than a nice pair of tits and a sexy ass."

Patriot's chuckle was as familiar as home. He sounded far too much like David. One of my best friends, and the scream I heard minutes before he died. The thought was sobering.

"Got a special girl worth taking my time and building something. She's it for me, man. My ol' lady is fucking fearless." I didn't miss the way his voice seemed to catch. "I miss David too."

My thoughts must have been obvious. "That's not why I'm here, though."

"Didn't think so." Patriot blew a cloud of smoke from his lungs, and it rose upward, hovering in the air above our heads. "My guess is it's something to do with that pretty little brunette you brought here with you."

It was hard to look Patriot in the eye for long. It was just like staring down his dead nephew, conjuring up images and memories I didn't want to haunt the rest of my evening.

"It does. I need a place to lay low. Not sure how long."

"Done. Before I take it to Grim, I need a little more info to go on."

"When I left the VA this afternoon, I found a young girl being beaten on the side of the road. Couldn't let that go, Dale."

"Shit. That the girl you brought with you?"

"Yeah."

"Who was beatin' on her?" Patriot looked pissed. I knew he hated that shit as much as I did.

"He was oddly familiar. I didn't realize who I'd shot until I was on my Harley and ridin' away with her on the back of my bike."

"Fuck. Tell me."

"Guy was sticking his boot up her ass," I fumed. "He kicked her fucking hard," I seethed. "Should have seen the way he smacked her and how hard she hit the ground. I saw the marks around her throat when he nearly choked her."

"Who?" Patriot had about as much patience as a rabid dog.

"Angel Mackenzie."

Patriot whistled low. "Grim isn't gonna like this."

"Yeah, I figured that. Not like I meant to start shit with the golden boy of the Guerrero Cartel. What the fuck was he doing in my neighborhood anyway?" I fumed.

"This is gonna stir up a hornet's nest, Flint. The club has to vote. I can't say for sure if you can stay here or not. Got to take it to my pres and then church."

"I understand." I really did. I'd grown up around several different clubs. It wasn't a surprise how things worked. The choice had to be a group decision, and every brother had a chance to weigh in. "If I need to leave, I won't hold it against you."

Patriot sighed. "That's just it. You're like family to me. Whatever the decision of the club, I'm going to have your back. Know that, Flint. You're a brother whether you wear the patch or not. I don't say that shit lightly."

"I know." I felt the same.

"You almost died trying to save David. Didn't forget what you lost or the scars that you carry."

All of the emotion buried deep within threatened to surface.

"What I'm sayin' is that you won't be going anywhere alone."

He wasn't going to risk his life for me. No fuckin' way. The more I thought about it, the more I realized I shouldn't have come here to begin with. I was placing Patriot, Grim, and the entire club at risk. If anyone noticed I was here, The Crossroads would be in danger.

"I shouldn't have come."

Patriot shot me a look. "Don't pull that shit with me. You're not leaving until I talk to Grim. Give me the night. That's all I ask. I'll let you know the decision in the morning."

Nodding, I didn't have any intention of sticking around.

"Fuckin' say it, Flint. I know you won't go back on your word if you give it."

He knew me too well. "Fine, Patriot. I won't leave before tomorrow."

"That means midnight, you slick fucker. Don't even try. I'll put a prospect on your ass and watch every move you make."

"Dammit, Dale. I'm not gonna leave. Okay?"

A triumphant smile curved his lips. "Now I know."

I flipped him off as he laughed and exited the room, the door shutting with a soft click. Kane was perched on his haunches, waiting for any word from me that he could move.

I shook my head. "Guard, Kane."

His dark eyes focused on me, but his ears perked up, listening for any hint of danger.

Now that I was alone, I could let the stress of the last few hours release. Picking up a glass from the bar, I filled it with whiskey and tossed the contents back. Three more followed it. My belly burned with the liquor, and I welcomed the distraction.

My thoughts were so scattered that I hardly noticed when the door opened, and I was no longer alone. A sweet, sexy voice brought me back to the present.

"You're drinking alone."

My head whipped in her direction, and I leaned against the bar, ticking my head in Lark's direction. "You're observant."

"Aw. Don't get all offended on my account." Lark snatched the glass from my hand, poured a shot, and drank the whiskey in one gulp. She hissed as it went down, catching my humored expression. "What? I have plenty of reasons to drink."

She sure did. No argument there.

"Pretty reckless to shoot Angel. You've got a target on your back now."

"Even more reckless to become indebted to the asshole," I fired back.

Having a target on my back wasn't anything new. Shit. Did she forget I was a Marine? Veteran or not, I wasn't afraid of that prick.

"Maybe I was lonely."

Scoffing, I shook my head. "No way. You wanted the attention, or you needed it. Maybe you craved the danger like it was some bad romance novel and hoped he'd take you to his mystery dungeon of toys. I don't get that vibe, though. I'm thinkin' you got roped into something too deep to dig your way out. Maybe for a family member or friend. Either way, you need to stay as far from Angel Mackenzie as you can get."

She refilled the glass and drank again, wiping the back of her hand across her mouth before she hiccupped. "I'm stupid, I guess." There was far too much sincerity in her tone.

No admittance but also no denial.

"Hey," I chided, crooking a finger under her chin to lift her face toward mine. "Don't ever call yourself stupid. I mean it."

For the first time, she let some of the vulnerability she felt rise to the surface. I knew what it meant for her to let me in. Hell, I was the fucking king of pushing people away. Lark didn't have to open up to me, but she did. She tore down a wall she could have kept there, and I would have understood that too. I could feel her insecurity as she stared into my eyes, and I didn't like it. She was too fucking fierce to let this get the best of her.

"He's going to kill me."

"Why would he want to harm you?" I tried to gentle my voice so she felt comfortable enough to confess the truth. Inside, I growled like a beast waiting to rip free and avenge her.

"I might have flushed his stash of meth down the toilet."

Uh-oh. "You messed with the man's drugs?" Incredulous, I couldn't believe she had the guts to get rid of a known drug dealer's product. "How much was it worth?"

She closed her eyes and blurted out her words, wincing at the number. "I flushed about five pounds or so. Angel said it was well over $100,000 in value."

She was fucking screwed. Angel and his thugs had killed for much less in the past. When I first came home after being discharged, the news had covered his suspected involvement in a drug bust, but nothing could be pinned on him. His daddy bailed him out.

Angel Mackenzie was a thug with an ego, and powerful men provided protection. His uncle Salazar was the muscle behind the Guerrero Cartel who moved meth and cocaine into the U.S. from Venezuela. Luis Guerrero was the old Spanish Don who ruled ruthlessly and without apology. He was also Salazar's father and Angel's grandfather.

What did this mean for the club? Patriot admitted they helped relocate shipments and provided extra muscle for a fee. I didn't think it was wise to do business with criminals like Salazar, but it wasn't my call. All I knew, Grim wanted out and had been trying to find a reason since his son was born.

I had to be careful. Didn't want to piss off Grim or the Royal Bastards, but I wasn't letting Angel get his hands on Lark again either. Fuck. I had less headaches dealing with shit overseas.

"I won't let them hurt you," I responded with conviction.

Bright green eyes shimmered with tears as they opened. "You can't promise that. You don't even know me, Flint. We met today, less than eight hours ago. How do you know I'm not lying? Or using you? Maybe I staged the whole thing."

"You took a beating to ride on the back of my Harley? That's fuckin' wild, little firecracker."

The words left my mouth with a seductive purr, softening the truth.

I'd do what I needed to keep her safe and away from Angel Mackenzie.

"No. I, uh, shit," she cursed, distracted by how I stared at her mouth. "You don't need to worry about my reasons."

She was too damn feisty. Sexy. Stubborn. A part of me wanted to see if I could tame such a wild little bird.

My head lowered, hovering only a few inches away from the pouty pink softness I remembered touching only an hour ago when we first arrived. That kiss lit a low flame inside me, and I couldn't stop wondering what it would feel like to slide my dick through those same silky lips.

Nothing good could come from this attraction that I felt. I was oddly protective and downright obsessed with the little minx. The idea of any other man taking advantage of her sweetness fired up a rage I hadn't felt since I left the Corps. My entire body tensed and pleaded for release.

She was the only way I'd lose some of this excess energy, and I wanted her warmth wrapped around me when I finally let down my walls for a brief moment. She made me want to feel again. It was fucking dangerous but also intoxicating.

My chin dropped another inch.

I just wanted one little taste. A single night. One chance.

This chemistry between us did wicked things to my brain. My fingers had been itching to touch her since the moment her sweet little ass dropped onto the seat of my bike. She'd been taken advantage of and abused, her trust broken, and for some reason, I wanted to prove to her that not every man would treat her that way. I could be gentle. Tender. Everything she wanted and needed.

The problem was, I knew it would only lead to craving her more. An itch that couldn't be tamed with just a few scratches. I knew this, but I couldn't walk away.

I didn't do relationships and didn't indulge feelings. My heart was untouchable. I locked it away and swore I wouldn't let anyone else in again. It hurt too fucking much.

Didn't change the fact that I wanted balls deep inside her and couldn't wait to hear that sexy voice crying out my name in pleasure.

"One night," I growled low, offering what I could give, as little as it was. "Say yes."

Her eyes locked on mine. She blinked.

"Say yes," I repeated, curling my hand around her neck, letting my palm rest against her throat as my thumb brushed her jaw.

Her body shifted closer to mine.

When her pulse thrummed, and I felt each beat of her heart as it quickened, I knew I had my answer.

Hell on Wheels is available to read now!

SNEAK PEEK

"**I**T DOESN'T HAVE TO be this way," Amelia reminded me, dropping her chin onto her fist as she gave me one of her enigmatic smiles, the kind that hinted she couldn't quite figure out the mystery I presented as she stared into my eyes. "You can still change your mind."

I didn't want to change my mind. My fingers tapped the old, worn wood of the bar stained with years of spills, chemicals, and body fluids. Everything from bar brawls to food fights had dumped debris onto the surface, and although it was cleaned daily, the wear wasn't fully disguised. Deep gouges in several spots proved not everyone used their fists when things got rowdy.

Still, the bar had character like my favorite pair of old slippers—comfy, familiar, and a little too worn. The scent of lemon and whiskey hung like a heavy curtain in the air, as comforting as home would ever be to me now, especially after the years I'd struggled on my own. Funny how smells conjured the past and evoked poignant memories of moments too far gone ever to bring back.

"Just give me another shot," I ordered, ignoring the brief flash of concern in her deep baby blues.

"You don't have to leave."

"Amelia," I began as she sighed, pushing off the bar to refill my glass.

"I don't want you to have a life full of regrets like me. There comes a time when you get too old to change the past. If you'd just—"

I cut her off, a bit flustered. "I need to do this."

"But so far away, Henny?"

"The farther, the better," I announced, trying not to dwell on all the shit of recent months. "It's time I tried to strike out on my own, live a little of life instead of sitting here, consumed by grief and everything I can't do to change it."

"I understand," she replied softly, "better than you know."

"I don't want to hurt anymore," I whispered, hating that ache in my chest that never diminished.

"Oh, baby. C'mere."

She rounded the bar, opening her arms as I slipped into her embrace, loving how she brought me in, closing out the problems of the world. Her hugs were magical. They had a way of healing hurts and restoring hope.

When I finally leaned back, she brushed a strand of my hair behind my ear, giving my shoulder a brief squeeze.

"I hate the idea of you leaving, even if it's only a short time."

"I know."

"Josie is going to be upset."

Shit. "I'll talk to her. She'll understand."

Amelia sighed. "We'll both understand and still hate it."

Now, I just felt guilty.

"Where will you go? What are you going to do for work?"

I already thought out the details. I could waitress or bartend since I had plenty of experience.

Amelia taught me everything I knew. "I'll find something."

"You sure you can't stay?"

The pleading expression on her face pulled at my heartstrings. If I remembered my mother and she was still alive, I'd hope she would be as kind and concerned as Amelia.

Few people cared about orphans or foster kids. I was only one of many. Without Amelia's intervention, I would never have made it this far.

Nearly fifteen years.

I owed her my life. She saved me from the streets after my last family tried to turn me out, charging men to come in and touch me, auctioning off my virginity at twelve to the highest bidder. If they found out the truth, I would have been beaten for risking their plan.

Late one night, I ran. The streets weren't a safe place for a young girl. I was lucky that I wasn't assaulted before Amelia found me one night a few weeks later, digging around in her dumpster behind the bar for something to eat.

"How will I ever learn to make it on my own?"

She hung her head, nodding. "You're right. You need to do this." She lifted her chin, giving me that bright, crooked smile that warmed my heart.

"Thank you."

Amelia's bar, The Rising Sun Tavern, was the first place I ever dared to call home. She welcomed me in, overlooked my filthy appearance, and gave me a second chance. I had a full belly, clean clothes, a roof over my head, and someone who actually cared whether I lived or died.

There was power in the feelings she evoked. Hope blossomed. My heart began to mend. Most of all, the broken, forgotten, discarded little girl started to trust again.

"You hungry?" she asked, heading toward the kitchen. "Josie's going to be in from school soon. You know how she's always starving. I'm going to make a snack."

"Cheese fries with ranch and Chicken tenders?"

She chuckled at my favorite meal. "Of course."

Amelia disappeared into the kitchen as I sat at the bar, my gaze sliding over the empty seats that would soon fill with patrons.

A bright L.E.D. sign hung above the entrance with two swinging doors where the bar's name lit up with a blazing neon orange sun.

The rest of the décor boasted more L.E.D. signs for liquor on the painted walls. Dozens of tables were scattered about with mismatched chairs, but the bar featured the best seats in the house. Those stools remained packed all night long.

The place was a little run down, but I wouldn't want it any other way. We touched it up with a new coat of paint every summer and tried to update what we could when Amelia earned extra cash. None of the customers ever complained about the décor or refused to enter the bar. Not that Amelia would bother listening to it.

The back door opened through the kitchen area, opposite the walk-in freezer, leading out to the dumpster. There wasn't much except for a rusted table and a couple of folding chairs that Amelia kept for the employees who smoked. The ashtray she added always overflowed, cigarette butts littering the table's worn surface. Most of the staff kept the trash cleaned up so the area didn't appear too cluttered.

"Mom! Henny! I'm home."

Josie's sweet voice shouted her greeting as she entered, not bothering to catch the back door before I heard it slam shut. She appeared a few seconds later, dropping her bag beside the bar and sighing loudly.

"What's the matter, Josie-bear?" I asked, using her favorite nickname.

"It happened again."

Shit. Was I supposed to know what she meant?

"Boys?"

She wrinkled her nose. "Eww. No." Her arm lifted, and my gaze fell on the discolored patches of skin. "The mean girls."

Little bitches. "I'm sorry, honey. It's not right they tease you."

"I can't help what my skin does," she exclaimed as her lower lip quivered. "I hate them."

"Awww. C'mere."

Josie's blue eyes filled with tears, and I hugged her, smoothing the long strands of her brown hair.

"It's rotten that they're such jerks. I know it's hard to put up with it every day."

"I tried to explain about vitiligo, but they didn't care." She swiped across her cheeks as she sat back on her stool. "They're stupid."

I let her have that since it was difficult enough not to lose my temper. What was the matter with those kids?

"I think you should talk to your mom," I announced as Amelia entered the bar, carrying a basket of chicken strips, cheese fries, and plenty of ranch.

She placed the food in front of me, casting a concerned glance at her daughter. "What happened?"

I gave Josie an encouraging smile. "Why don't I eat, and you both go talk? I'll finish things up here, Amelia."

"Okay." Josie hopped off the stool and followed her mother into the kitchen as I picked up a fry, dipping it in the ranch before taking a bite. I shouldn't have skipped breakfast. Starving, I ate every bite, tossing the trash and leaving the empty basket on top of the bar.

I spent the next twenty minutes preparing to open, breezing through the checklist. Amelia still wasn't back, and I decided not to bother her, unlocking the front door for customers. She knew I could handle things without her until it became too busy.

Skeet would be here soon to help with security while Ned started his shift in the kitchen. Since this was only a weekday afternoon, no additional staff tended the bar or made drinks.

Amelia and I handled the nightly rush without a problem.

Bored, I picked up a washcloth, wiping down the bar, tables, and frequently touched surfaces, ensuring the place appeared clean.

The front door swung open as I glanced over, revealing four men I had never seen before tonight. Four strangers who didn't belong here and certainly didn't show up just to try the new beer on tap. All four wore leather vests, jeans, and boots. Silver chains dangled from a couple of belt loops, but the guns they didn't bother to hide caught my attention the most.

Bikers. The wild type. They looked like determined, mean motherfuckers too. Outlaws. One-percenter motorcycle club members.

Shit.

Not a single one of them was scrawny. In fact, they all resembled pro wrestlers or bodybuilders. Bulging muscles, broad shoulders that tapered to trim abdomens, and not an ounce of fat. Not to mention plenty of dark tattoos.

They didn't hesitate, walking inside like they could do what they pleased. They spread out, quick to block any exit, sharp gazes quickly assessing the interior for hidden dangers.

Two of them were giants, ducking to avoid slamming their heads into the door as they entered. One with long dark hair that brushed his shoulders, stick straight and thick, wearing a skeletal mask over his face. He wore all black leather, any small bits of exposed skin covered in dark ink.

The other, a handsome and rugged type that reminded me of a Viking, had reddish-blond hair and multiple braids swept back beyond the shaved sides of his head. A long beard helped conceal his features, but something about his eyes made me shiver.

One of the four, probably the leader, stepped forward with his assertive expression and plenty of confidence. A patch labeled *president* adhered to the front of his vest.

His black hair was slicked back and slightly tousled, begging for someone to tidy the strands. I noted the style, longer on top and short on the sides, fading in that fresh-cut way you only saw right after a visit to the barber. His dark beard added a rough but attractive hint of rebellion.

Not that a biker obeyed the law or even cared about following rules. Of the four, his clothes were the most wrinkle-free and crisp.

The president remained silent, his gaze roaming over me as if waiting on something.

The fourth one, wearing a cowboy hat over shaggy brown hair, boots with spurs, faded, ripped jeans, and a playful smirk, strode my way with a swagger none of his friends could have pulled off. Golden skin dotted with a few tattoos, cleanshaven, and flashing a panty-melting grin, he appeared the least rough of the bunch. Warm, soft brown eyes revealed a touch of humor before he winked. "Who're you, darlin'?"

"Not now, Cowboy," the president ordered in an authoritative tone.

Cowboy? Not very original, but it fit.

The president approached, and I didn't back away, refusing to show fear or weakness as he closed in. I'd be stupid not to be afraid of these men. They were obviously dangerous, but I wouldn't be intimidated in the only place I called home. My chin lifted, waiting for him to say why they entered Amelia's bar. I never saw her interact with bikers.

The big, dark one wearing the mask stayed silent. The shade of his eyes was disguised by the ghostly skull, and I wondered what color they'd be. His neck was the only area of his body uncovered beside his wrists and forearms. A tattoo of a black spider and web connected with a snake baring his fangs, winding around his throat. Hands clenched at his hips; his veiny forearms flexed briefly.

I could feel his hostility from here.

The snug black t-shirt he wore clung in all the right places, indenting at his pecs and chiseled abs. His biceps pushed the cloth up his arms, almost too large to be covered.

The tight jeans he wore molded to his thighs and drew my appreciation, but my attention returned to his hands, curious about the chunky silver rings on his fingers, slightly below the tattooed letters on each hand. LOST on the right and SOUL on the left. For some reason, I felt sad for him.

When he noticed I stared, a growl vibrated low in his throat.

"Reaper," the president warned.

Reaper. A name that fit this dark, chiseled man who seemed carved from obsidian straight out of hell.

"Is Amelia here?"

I didn't answer or reveal that I knew her. "Who are you?"

Reaper snarled beneath the mask, stalking forward.

The president held up his hand, halting Reaper's progress. "A valid question. I'm Devil, the president of the Reaper's Vale MC. These are some of my officers. My V.P. Raiden," he ticked his head toward the Viking who stood to his left, watching me intently, "my S.A.A. Reaper," nodding to the one in the mask who wouldn't stand still, "and my Treasurer, Cowboy."

I nodded, deciding I could be civil. "I'm Henrietta, but I go by Henny."

Devil smiled, intending to appear friendly, but I caught the calculating look that entered his pale blue eyes. "Thrilled to meet you, Henny." He cleared his throat, all business now. "I need to speak to Amelia. It's important. Is she around tonight?" The way he asked didn't leave doubt that he knew she never took a night off. She was too much of a control freak, and almost everyone in town could confirm it. Amelia had a reputation as a smart, shrewd, dedicated business owner. She needed a vacation but would never take one.

"What can I do for you?" Amelia asked, appearing before I had a chance to lie.

I didn't see Josie and hoped Amelia would send her upstairs to my apartment.

I had lived above the bar since the day I turned eighteen. A gift from Amelia at graduation, swearing a young woman needed her own place to start off on the right foot and prepare for the future. Josie had a spare key. At eleven, she was smart enough to listen when things got rowdy down here.

"You have something that belongs to us," Devil began, gesturing to one of the tables. "I'd like to talk about it."

Talk? *Sure.* My shoulders tensed as I watched Amelia sit across from Devil. I didn't believe these bikers were only here to talk.

Reaper paced the room, prowling closer as he circled the tables and chairs, constantly looking around the room. His gaze kept jumping from the windows to the door to the kitchen. I tried to ignore him, but he hissed at me when I moved a couple of stools away.

"What could I possibly have that belongs to a motorcycle club?"

Devil cleared his throat as if he wanted a drink. "You have a package. I believe Homer left it in your possession."

Amelia startled. "A package?"

"Yes," he replied impatiently. "It's quite valuable. We need it returned immediately."

Amelia's eyes blinked rapidly. "I don't know what package you think Homer gave me. I haven't seen him in months."

Raiden tsked, shaking his head.

Cowboy pulled out a cigarette, lit the end, and took a long drag. "Not smart to lie."

Reaper moved closer to Devil.

"Then you owe the club a debt."

Amelia sat back against her seat, disbelief visible on her face. "How much is this package worth? I can pay you."

189

"No!" Devil snarled. "It's priceless."

"I don't know what to give you!"

"Then you pay the debt back to the club how we see fit." His head ticked toward the scary one, and Reaper lunged in my direction, tugging me into his arms. "We'll take the girl as collateral. When your memory returns, call me."

Um, what!?

Amelia rushed to her feet, her voice panicked. "I don't know what you're talking about!" The high-pitched tone made me wonder if she lied. "You can't take Henny!"

"We can do whatever the fuck we want," Raiden announced.

Reaper chuckled. The deep, menacing tone vibrated in my chest, uncurling with dark promise.

"Henny." Amelia's voice sounded strained.

"I'll be okay. I promise." A stupid thing to say since I couldn't guarantee shit. All I knew was that I wouldn't risk these bikers harming Amelia or Josie.

Devil rose to his feet, heading toward the exit. His features twisted into a scowl, and he pushed open the swinging doors.

Reaper shoved me in front of him, not allowing a chance for me to say another word. Behind us, Cowboy and Raiden followed.

Outside, I nearly fought Reaper's grasp but decided to wait as I spotted the four motorcycles parked in a row.

Hiding the tremble in my hands, I clenched them tight against my hips, trying not to think about what would happen in the hours looming ahead.

"You still got that rope, Reaper?" Devil asked.

A silent nod followed from my captor.

"Tie her up."

Reaper's lips twitched with a dark grin, not bothering to suppress the enjoyment he received with the order.

Shit.

There was no point in running. I'd never get far and that didn't help Amelia or Josie. No, I had to see this through. Heaving a deep breath, I sighed.

I was fucked.

Twisted Iron is available to read now!

ABOUT THE AUTHOR

Nikki Landis is a romance enthusiast, tea addict, and book hoarder. She's the USA Today Bestselling Author of over fifty novels, including her widely popular Tonopah, NV RBMC series. She writes wickedly fierce, spicy romances featuring dirty talkin' bikers, deadly, overprotective reapers, wild bad boys, and the feisty, independent women they love. She's a mom to six sons, two of them Marines. Books are her favorite escape.

Nikki also writes monster and sci-fi romance under the pen name Synna Star. She lives in Ohio with her husband, boys, and a little Yorkie who really runs the whole house.

Made in the USA
Las Vegas, NV
10 February 2024

85632581R00121